THE GRAVE

DAN FRAGA

Become our fan on Facebook facebook.com/idwpublishing
Follow us on Twitter @idwpublishing
Subscribe to us on YouTube youtube.com/idwpublishing
See what's new on Tumblr tumblr.idwpublishing.com
Check us out on Instagram instagram.com/idwpublishing

IDW
www.IDWPUBLISHING.com

Chris Ryall, President, Publisher, & CCO
John Barber, Editor-In-Chief
Robbie Robbins, EVP & Sr. Art Director
Cara Morrison, Chief Financial Officer
Matthew Ruzicka, Chief Accounting Officer
David Hedgecock, Associate Publisher
Jerry Bennington, VP of New Product Development
Lorelei Bunjes, VP of Digital Services
Justin Eisinger, Editorial Director, Graphic Novels & Collections
Eric Moss, Sr. Director, Licensing & Business Development

Ted Adams, IDW Founder

ISBN: 978-1-68405-511-1   22 21 20 19   1 2 3 4

For international rights, contact licensing@idwpublishing.com

Dan Fraga Instagram @couchdoodles

THE GRAVE

STORY & ART
DAN FRAGA

COLLECTION DESIGNER
CLAUDIA CHONG

EDITOR
SCOTT DUNBIER

Well, hey, I gotta ask, does anybody actually *read* these introductions? If you've picked this up, that means you've either heard about *The Grave* somehow, or that you know my comics work and wanted to see what I've been up to since I left the medium in 2002. Either way, I thank you for picking this book up.

For the most part, my career has been spent drawing comic books, creating storyboards for movies, and directing animation. One of the things I am not known for is writing. Sure, I've plotted a few yarns, and contributed ideas on stories, but I've never written an entire story soup to nuts—until now. I've always wanted to write and draw something personal but I could never find the time. But I would jot down ideas that would go into a notebook, gathering dust as the years went by.

Those notes and story ideas would occasionally resurface in my brain but my old excuse of not having enough time would pop up. I'd say to myself, "I'll take some time off," or "during a holiday break." Alas, these opportunities never materialized in a way that worked. So, you might ask, how did I finally end up creating the book you're holding in your hands? Well, since you've made it this far, I'll tell you.

Friendships are important to everyone, of course, and I'm no exception. I have several stories in my notebooks that focus on relationships with friends, and how people interact together. There are many elements in *The Grave* that, at their core, are loosely based on people and incidents in my life... friendships. My best pals in my school days were Mike, Pete, Danny, and Billy. We'd have conversations about comics, Sci-Fi and our love of movies like *Stand by Me*, *Star Wars*, *Gremlins*, and *Back to the Future*. From 8th grade through high-school graduation, we were inseparable. I am who I am, in large part, because of those guys.

Another element of the story relates to my obsession with time, and how I remember points of my life through experiences, music, and places. My hometown of Martinez plays a role in *The Grave* (though I changed the name to Ashland). My grandparents' house is where Billy lives. Case's corner store is where we bought comics and candy. The throne is a real place in the hills of Martinez. I love where I grew up, and I remember those times with fondness.

You may be asking, "What do these elements have to do with actually finding the time to tell a full story?" It's simple: Passion. I was passionate enough about this story, it gnawed at my soul for *so* long, that I eventually *had* to tell it. I had a full-time job at Mattel animating cartoons—a three-hour commute—and a wife and three kids at home. Time wasn't something I had a lot of! Then I stumbled across a book by Steven Pressfield called *The War of Art*.

Pressfield, in his book, talks about the very problem I was having—being a creative person without time—but also about having no regrets. We, as creative people, must create the things yearning to be created, or, if not, we'll be filled with regret. But the one concept that struck me the most was the idea of creating something big incrementally, one day at a time. Instead of wishing for a large block of time to *eventually* create, use the time that you do have to create *now*. *Even if it's only 15 minutes a day*. And it dawned on me that I needed to *make* time—so for one year I woke up three hours earlier than normal, and in that time I would write, pencil, and ink one panel per day... and I could tell a story over the course of one year, in 365 panels.

I suddenly felt the freedom to release my passion into the world! That passion drove me day in and day out. Rain or shine. Whether sick or traveling. I drew a panel every single day for a year. The book you're holding is a representation of my passion. I hope you enjoy the story you're about to read and, even more, I hope you're inspired to tell your own stories, even if it's one day at a time.

Dan Fraga
February 2019

Photo by Phred Jackson.

1950

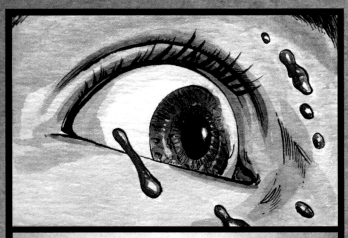

"BACK TO *HELL* WITH YOU! YOU *DEMON!!!*"

"NOOOOOooooooo!!!!!!!!"

"OH GOD."

EMMETT!!!
EMMETT!!!
EMMETT!!!
EMMETT!!!

"The fear of death follows from the fear of life. A man who lives fully is prepared to die at any time."

-Mark Twain

SUNDAY, SEPTEMBER 3, 1989. ASHLAND, USA.

"*BILLY,* DID YOU MAKE SURE TO PACK ENOUGH SOCKS?!" HIS MOTHER ASKS WITH GENUINE CONCERN.

"YES, MOM," BILLY REPLIES. "I'M *14* YEARS OLD. I'M GONNA BE A FRESHMAN IN *TWO* DAYS! ...*YEESH!*"

"WELL, I JUST DON'T WANT YOU TO BE EMBARRASSED IN FRONT OF YOUR FRIENDS..." MOM CONTINUES. "YOU JUST NEVER EVER KNOW, YOU KNOW?"

"YUP, YOU NEVER KNOW..." BILLY MUMBLES AS HE PACKS A STACK OF COMICS INTO HIS BACKPACK. "SOCKS ARE WHERE IT'S AT. *YEESH!* YOU ACT LIKE I WAS *10* YEARS OLD..."

"OH, LOOK, YOUR BUDDIES ARE HERE! HAVE A GREAT TIME PLAYING ARMY MAN..." MOM SAYS WITH A MOM TONE. "DON'T LET THE RUSKIES GET YOU! HEH. OH, AND STAY WARM."

"*HA!* ALL RIGHT, *MOM*. PLEASE TELL DAD I SAID 'BYE' AND THAT I'LL BE HOME IN TIME TO HELP HIM WITH THE BBQ TOMORROW."

BILLY HEADS DOWN THE PORCH STEPS TOWARD HIS TWO BEST PALS, MIKE AND PETE. THE THREE HAVE BEEN INSEPARABLE SINCE THIRD GRADE. HE DOES HIS BEST TO HIDE HIS EXCITEMENT FOR THEIR TRIP AHEAD.

" *WHAT'S UP, FELLAS!?* YOU READY TO DO THIS?"

"*HECK YEAH!*" MIKE SAYS, STOKED. "*HELLA READY!*" PETE EXCITEDLY ADDS.

"*GENTLEMEN*, WE *NEED* TO REMEMBER AND *SAVOR* THIS MOMENT," BILLY SAYS REVERENTLY... "THESE NEXT *TWO DAYS* WILL BE OUR LAST AS *'BOYS;'* AFTER THAT, WE'VE GOT *HIGH SCHOOL* TO LOOK FORWARD TO --"

" *-- AND THE CHICKS!*" MIKE REMINDS THE GUYS WITH SERIOUSNESS.

"*THAT*... AND AVOIDING BEING STUFFED INTO TRASH CANS..." PETE CAUTIONS.

THE BOYS CONTINUE ON THEIR JOURNEY. EVENTUALLY THE CONVERSATION ENDS UP WHERE IT ALWAYS DOES; *COMICS*.

"...THEN IT'S SETTLED, *BYRNE* IS BETTER THAN *PEREZ*," BILLY DECLARES.

"AND LET US NOT FORGET *FRANK MILLER*," MIKE ADDS.

"C'MON GUYS, MILLER IS IN A DIFFERENT LEAGUE. THOSE GUYS ARE *POP*, MILLER IS *NOIR*. APPLES TO ORANGES," PETE SAYS, MATTER-OF-FACTLY.

THE BOYS HEAD INTO *CASE'S*, THE NEIGHBORHOOD CORNER STORE.

CASE'S IS A WORLD OF JOY AND FANTASY FOR A YOUNG MAN, AND THE BOYS WASTE NO TIME TO INDULGE IN THEIR FAVORITE ACTIVITY. FOR A BRIEF FEW MINUTES, THE ONLY SOUNDS THAT CAN BE HEARD ARE THE OLD RADIO IN THE BACK ROOM, THE HUM OF THE ICE CREAM FREEZER NEAR THE REGISTER AND THE FLIPPING OF COMIC BOOK PAGES. AFTER A FULL PERUSAL OF THE SPINNER RACK, THE BOYS STOCK UP ON SNACKS, SODA, BOLOGNA, AND A FEW OTHER THINGS. THE GUYS' LAST ADVENTURE AS *"BOYS"* IS OFF TO A GREAT START.

LATER, ON THE TRAIN TRACKS...

"THINK ABOUT IT," MIKE SAYS. "THERE ARE INVISIBLE FREQUENCIES AROUND US. MICROWAVES, RADIO WAVES, AND OTHER WAVES. WE USE TUNERS TO HEAR AND USE WAVES AT OUR WILL WHY WOULDN'T IT BE THE SAME FOR LIGHT FREQUENCIES? I'VE SEEN STUFF WITH MY POLARIZED GLASSES FOR INSTANCE; THEY'RE A SIMPLE TUNER FOR LIGHT. WHAT WOULD HAPPEN IF WE COULD TUNE INTO DIFFERENT KINDS OF FREQUENCIES? WOULD WE SEE OTHER DIMENSIONS? COULD WE SEE NEW COLORS?"

"DUDE, WHAT IF YOU SEE CREATURES AND THEY ATTACK YOU?" BILLY ASKS IN ALL SERIOUSNESS.

"THINK ABOUT IT," BILLY CONTINUES. "LET'S SAY THEY MAKE YOUR TUNER IT'S A VIRTUAL REALITY THING, RIGHT? YOU GO THERE, YOU PUT THE THING ON, AND THEY START TUNING YOU INTO SOME NEW SHIT. THINGS YOU'VE NEVER SEEN START POPPING UP. SCARY SHIT. AND THAT'S WHEN THEY COME... *THE CREATURES FROM ANOTHER DIMENSION!* AT FIRST YOU'RE LIKE ALL 'HECK YEAH!' *BUT THEN...*"

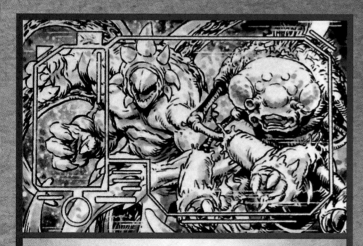

"...THAT'S WHEN IT GETS *REAL* CRAZY. THE CREATURES *SEE YOU!!* OF COURSE THEY'RE GONNA WANT TO CHECK YOU OUT, MAYBE DO SOME PROBING OF THE *UNWELCOME* KIND, OR EVEN WORSE; THEY FIGURE OUT A WAY TO GET INTO YOUR *MIND*... THEY *INFECT* YOU," BILLY GOES ON. "IT WOULDN'T BE ANYTHING LIKE YOU'D EXPECT EITHER. IT'D BE SILENT, BUT THE INSIDE OF YOUR MIND WOULD BE *SCREAMING*... "

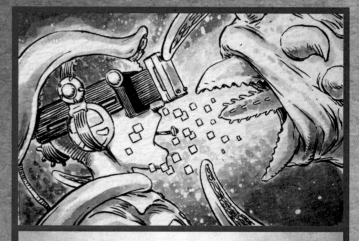

"ONCE THEY'RE IN THERE, THERE'S NO GOING BACK," BILLY WARNS. "THEY PERFORM A MIND-MELD LIKE *VENOM* FROM *SPIDER-MAN*, BUT IT'S A ONE WAY STREET; *YOU BECOME IT.* YOU'RE NO LONGER YOU. YOU'RE INFECTED. THEN YOU COME BACK TO THE REAL WORLD WITH THE CONTAGION AND YOU SPREAD IT LIKE A BAD COLD. ONE BY ONE, SOCIETY FALLS. *WE BECOME...*"

" ...SPACE ZOMBIES!!!! "

"AND WHEN THE *SPACE FLU* IS DONE WITH US," BILLY CONCLUDES. "WE ALL TURN ON EACH OTHER. *BOOM!* THE END OF THE HUMAN RACE."

MIKE LOOKS AT BILLY WITH INCREDULITY. "YOU'VE GOT IT ALL *WRONG*. WHEN YOU HEAR SOMETHING ON THE RADIO OR ANY SORT OF BROADCAST, YOU'RE NOT HEARING THE THING MAKE THE *ACTUAL SOUND*. YOU'RE NOT NEXT TO *THE THING*. YOU'RE HEARING A TRANSMISSION. A REPRESENTATION. YOU CAN'T TOUCH IT. IT'S IMPOSSIBLE. IT'D BE THE SAME THING WITH THE VIRTUAL REALITY THINGY. EVEN IF THERE *WERE* CREATURES, THEY COULDN'T TOUCH YOU. *EVER*. QUANTUM PHYSICS."

"MAN, HOW DO YOU COME UP WITH THIS *SHIT?*" BILLY ASKS..

"DUDE, IT WAS ON *STAR TREK!* C'MON. BESIDES, IT ISN'T *VR*. IT WOULD BE *HYPER-REALITY*. IT WOULD BE *"MORE REALITY"*," MIKE CLARIFIES.
"THINK ABOUT THE PEOPLE THE FIRST TIME THEY HEARD RADIO. WHAT MUST HAVE *THAT* BEEN LIKE? BEFORE THAT MAYBE THE PHONOGRAPH... BUT BEFORE THAT, THE ONLY SOUND YOU HEARD WERE *AS THEY WERE HAPPENING: LIVE*. SO THAT'S WHAT *YOUR EXAMPLE* WOULD BE LIKE."

"WELL, THAT'S MY POINT, DUDE." SAYS BILLY

"WHAT DO YOU MEAN?" ASKS MIKE.

"I'M SAYING, USING YOUR DESCRIPTION: IF YOU'RE LOOKING AT THESE THINGS IN THE TUNER," BILLY CLARIFIES. "AND THE VOLUME WAS UP, YOU CAN GET BLINDED WITH WHAT THAT ENERGY CAN DO. WHAT IT DOES. MAYBE IT COULD EVEN POSSESS YOU, LIKE I SAID"

"WELL, IF THAT'S THE CASE," SAYS MIKE. "THEN IT CAN BE CONTAINED."

ALL OF A SUDDEN, PETE BREAKS HIS SILENCE.

"*GUYS,* YOU *DO* KNOW WHAT YOU'RE TALKING ABOUT, DON'T YOU?
THIS IS FUCKING *GHOSTBUSTERS,* MAN.
IT'S GHOSTBUSTERS!
IT'S GHOSTS. YOU GUYS ARE TALKING ABOUT *GHOSTS!*"

BWAHHAHAHAHAHAHAHAHAHAHA!!

"HEH, HEH. DAMN, PETE, YOU ARE *SO RIGHT,*" BILLY GAINS HIS COMPOSURE.
"OK, LET'S GET GOING. THE SPOT IS JUST OVER THESE HILLS. LET'S GET THERE AND GET SET UP BEFORE IT GETS DARK. I DON'T WANNA BE TRYING TO SET UP CAMP IN PITCH BLACKNESS. *KNOW WHAT I'M SAYIN'?*"

"WORD," SAYS MIKE.

"NO JOKE," CHIMES PETE.

THE BOYS MAKE THEIR WAY UP THE HILL TOWARDS 'THE SPOT', BUT NOT BEFORE PETE HAS A REQUEST.

"*DUDE*, BILLY, TELL US ANOTHER ONE OF YOUR *SPACE-GUY* STORIES!"

"IT'S '*ASTRO-KNIGHT*', YOU KNOW, LIKE '*ASTRONAUT*'," BILLY CLARIFIES.

"YOU MEAN, '*SPACE KNIGHT*', LIKE *ROM?*" MIKE CORRECTS.

"*YEAH*, LIKE *ROM*," BILLY EYE ROLLS. "SO, ANYWAY, THIS *SPACE-KNIGHT*..." BILLY CONTINUES.

" ...HE'S A REAL *BADASS!* HE'S JUST GOT FINISHED WITH SOME REAL HEROIC SPACE SHIT," BILLY SAYS WITH CONVICTION. "AND HE'S *VERY, VERY* THIRSTY. HE WALKS FOR HALF A DAY BEFORE HE COMES TO A SMALL SPACE TOWN... "

" ...THIS PLACE IS A REAL *SHITHOLE*. IT LOOKS A LOT LIKE *MOS EISLEY*: '*A WRETCHED HIVE OF SCUM AND VILLAINY*,' AS THEY SAY. IT'S ALSO GOT A *CANTINA*. WHAT MAKES THIS CANTINA DIFFERENT, IS THAT IT'S GOT A SIGN OUT FRONT THAT READS '*FREE BEER*.' NOW REMEMBER, OUR HERO, THE ASTRO-KNIGHT IS VERY *VERY THIRSTY* FROM ALL OF THAT SPACE HERO SHIT HE WAS DOING, SO HE HEADS RIGHT INTO THAT CANTINA FOR HIS FREE BEER."

"*BARTENDER!* I'LL HAVE MY *FREE BEER* NOW! IN FACT; WHY WASTE TIME? I'LL TAKE *TWO* BEERS RIGHT AWAY!" THE ASTRO-KNIGHT SAYS WITH A THIRSTY BRAVADO.

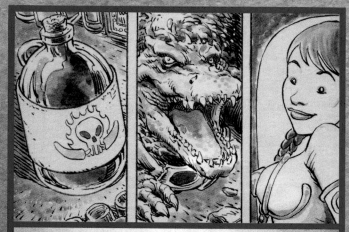

THE WHOLE CANTINA ERUPTS IN LAUGHTER. ALIENS FROM AROUND THE GALAXY POINT AND SNICKER AT THE ASTRO-KNIGHT.

"*SURE!* WHY NOT *FOUR BEERS?*" THE BARTENDER ASKS SARCASTICALLY. "YOU LOOK THIRSTY. I'LL GET TO POURING 'EM, BUT FIRST YOU'VE GOTTA PASS *THE TEST.*"

THE PLACE ERUPTS AGAIN.

"*THE TEST?*..." THE ASTRO-KNIGHT ASKS CONFUSED.

"IF YA WANT FREE BEER FOR LIFE, *YES*, THERE'S A TEST." THE BARTENDER CONTINUES. "*FIRST*, YA GOTTA DRINK THIS JUG OF *PEPPERED SPACE TEQUILA*. IT'S SUPER FUCKING HOT, AND *YA CAN'T SPILL A DROP*. SECOND, THERE'S A *SPACE-CROC* DOWNSTAIRS WITH A *SORE TOOTH*. YA GOTTA PULL IT OUT WITH YOUR *BARE HANDS*. THIRD AND LAST, THERE'S A SPACE-BROTHEL UPSTAIRS, AND THERE'S A GIRL WHO'S NEVER BEEN SATISFIED *IN THAT WAY*. (*IF YA KNOW WHAT I MEAN.*) YA GOTTA GO UP THERE AND *ROCK HER WORLD*. AFTER COMPLETING *ALL THREE* OF THOSE TASKS: *FREE BEER FOR LIFE.*"

"*DAMN*," SIGHS THE ASTRO-KNIGHT, COMPLETELY DEFLATED." I *AM* REALLY THIRSTY AND THE PROSPECT OF *FREE BEER FOR LIFE* SOUNDS SO ENTICING, *BUT SHIT*, THOSE TASKS JUST GET HARDER TO DO AS THEY GO. I'LL JUST TAKE A SPACE-WHISKEY ON THE ROCKS INSTEAD. *MAKE IT A DOUBLE.*"

TWO HOURS AND *FIVE DOUBLE SPACE-WHISKEYS* LATER, THE ASTRO-KNIGHT STARTS TO RECONSIDER HIS STANCE ON THE FREE BEER CHALLENGE. IN FACT, HE'S FORMED THE IDEA IN HIS HEAD THAT THE CHALLENGE IS HIS NEW *NEMESIS*. HE EYEBALLS THE *PEPPERED SPACE TEQUILA* WITH DRUNKEN CONFIDENCE AND CALCULATES HIS *FIRST MOVE*...

"*LET'S* FUCKING DO TH*IS!!!*"

The *ASTRO-KNIGHT* GRABS THE *PEPPERED SPACE TEQUILA* AND STARTS TO CHUG WITH THE DETERMINATION OF A MAN WHO HAS BEATEN A *HORDE OF D'HFUKAI BADGERS* WITH HIS *BARE HANDS*. THE HEAT FROM THE TEQUILA IS *SO INTENSE*, THE ASTRO-KNIGHT SHEDS A TEAR. WHAT HE DOES *NOT* DO: *SPILL A SINGLE DROP.*

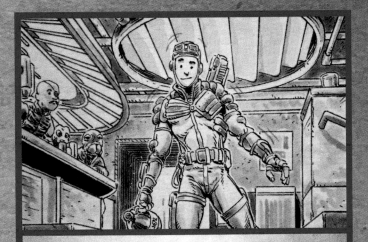

THE ASTRO-KNIGHT STANDS, WOBBLES, THEN STEELS HIS COMPOSURE. *NOTHING* WILL STOP HIM FROM GETTING HIS *FREE BEER*, NOT EVEN HIS NEXT CHALLENGE: *THE SPACE-CROC!!!*

HOLDING ON TO THE RAIL, THE ASTRO-KNIGHT MANAGES HIS WAY DOWN THE STAIRS TO THE *SPACE-CROC*. THE PATRONS OF THE CANTINA LOOK ON IN *COMPLETE DISBELIEF. HE MAY JUST PULL THIS OFF!*

AT FIRST IT'S *EERILY QUIET*.
THE PATRONS HAVE TO LEAN IN TO *HEAR* ANYTHING.
BUT THEN--

--THE ASTRO-KNIGHT LETS OUT A *BLOOD-CURDLING SCREAM*, THEN THE
SPACE-CROC LETS OUT A *DEAFENING ROAR*, THEN THERE'S A LOUD

THUMP!

AND THEN... *SILENCE*.

AFTER A *LONG* MOMENT, THE ASTRO-KNIGHT SLOWLY LIMPS HIS WAY UP
THE STAIRS. THE CANTINA PATRONS LOOK ON, *ASTONISHED*.

THE ASTRO-KNIGHT STANDS TRIUMPHANT. HE'S *BATTERED*, HE'S *BLOODY*,
BUT HE'S READY FOR THE *FINAL CHALLENGE*. HE STEADIES HIMSELF AS HE
PROCLAIMS--

"NOW, SHOW ME THE WAY TO THE LADY WITH **THE SORE TOOTH!!!**"

"PFFFFFFFT!!" MIKE SPITS OUT HIS SODA.

"GET IT?!" BILLY ASKS, AS THE BOYS CONTINUE THEIR WALK TO THE *'SPOT'*.

*"WAIT... THE **ASTRO-KNIGHT**, HE--HE **BANGED** THE **SPACE-CROC?!**"* PETE ASKS IN ALL SERIOUSNESS.

"PETE, YOUR POWERS OF PERCEPTION HAVE LEFT ME *STUNNED!"* BILLY JOKES.
"YES, THE CROC GOT A GOOD HELPING OF THAT *SPACE-LOVIN'.* NOW, *C'MON,* THE SPOT SHOULD BE RIGHT UP HERE, OVER THIS HILL... "

" YEP," BILLY CONFIRMS. *" THERE IT IS--"*

"--THE SPOT..."

"OH, SNAP!!" EXCLAIMS MIKE. "IT'S BADASS. IT LOOKS MAGICAL!"

"UH, WHAT'S WITH THE PILE OF ROCKS?" PETE QUIZZES.

"THAT 'PILE OF ROCKS'," BILLY ANSWERS. "IS A THRONE!"

"WHERE DID IT COME FROM?!" MIKE ASKS.

"NOT SURE, NOBODY REALLY KNOWS..." BILLY SAYS, PONDERING.

"WELL, HOW'D YOU HEAR ABOUT THIS PLACE?" PETE INQUIRES.

"IT'S BEEN A FEW YEARS," BILLY ANSWERS. "MY FOLKS USED TO TAKE ME UP HERE WHEN I WAS A KID. WE'D COME UP AND RUN THE DOGS. I ASKED MY MOM ABOUT THE THRONE, AND SHE TOLD ME THAT HER MOM SHOWED IT TO HER WHEN SHE WAS LITTLE, BUT THAT SHE DIDN'T REMEMBER MUCH ELSE ABOUT IT."

"YEAH, WELL, I'LL TELL YOU WHAT I KNOW ABOUT IT," MIKE SAYS WITH GLEE. "THIS THRONE IS THE CAPTAIN'S CHAIR! MAKE IT SO, NUMBER ONE!"

THE BOYS START TO UNPACK, AND GET READY FOR THE NIGHT AHEAD.

"ALL RIGHT, WHO'S READY FOR SOME OF *RICHIE'S PAL, BOBBLEHEAD?*" BILLY ASKS AS HE PROUDLY PULLS THE ISSUE FROM HIS BACKPACK.

THE OTHER BOYS GROAN WITH THEIR DISAPPOINTMENT.

"*REALLY*, DUDE? *BOBBLEHEAD?!*" MIKE REPLIES.

"NOT *BOBBLEHEAD...* " ADDS PETE.

"PERHAPS, YOU *GENTLEMEN* WOULD PREFER... *BOOBS* INSTEAD." BILLY FLIPS THE COMIC COVER TO REVEAL A NUDIE MAGAZINE.

"*HOLY SMOKES DUDE, SMUT!!*" MIKE SAYS, EXCITEDLY.

"*YES, MAMS!*" REPLIES BILLY.

"WHOA, *DUDE*, HOW'D YOU GET *THAT?*" PETE ASKS, WITH SERIOUS CURIOSITY.

"YEAH, MAN, *DO TELL...* " MIKE ADDS.

"WELL, I FOUND WHERE MY POPS STASHES THE *GOOD STUFF.*" SAYS BILLY. "THERE'S ALL KINDS OF STUFF IN THERE. MY FOLKS EVEN HAVE SOME *X-RATED MOVIES* ON *BETAMAX*. FREAKY STUFF. ANYWAY, I SNUCK *THIS* IN ONE OF MY COMICS, AND POPPED IT IN MY BAG. THEY WERE NONE THE WISER."

"AH, *MAN!* YA GONNA *BOP THAT BOLOGNA?!*" SNAPS MIKE.

"*HAMMER THAT HAM?!*" BILLY RETORTS.

"*POUND THAT PASTRA--*" MIKE SAYS, INTERRUPTED.

"UH, *GUYS--*" SAYS PETE, STOPPING THE FUNNY TRAIN.

"--I'M ALL ABOUT *LUNCHMEAT ALLITERATION* AND ALL, BUT... NEED I REMIND YOU THAT IT'S GONNA GET DARK *REAL SOON?*" PETE CAUTIONS. "AND *SPEAKING* OF *LUNCHMEAT;* I SAY WE GET A *FIRE* GOING AND WE FRY UP THIS FINE BOLOGNA! *I'M FUCKING HUNGRY!*"

"*GOOD CALL*, DUDE." SAYS BILLY. "YOU PACK THAT CAMPING SHOVEL?"

PETE PULLS THE CAMPING SHOVEL FROM HIS BACKPACK AND HANDS IT OVER TO BILLY. BILLY STARTS TO DIG THE HOLE TO BUILD THE FIRE IN. PERFECT TIMING TOO. THE SUN WAS STARTING TO SET, AND FAST.

AS BILLY CONTINUES TO DIG, HIS THOUGHTS BEGIN TO WANDER INTO INTROSPECTION. HE BEGINS TO THINK ABOUT THE SUMMER PAST, AND HOW IN A FEW DAYS HE AND HIS BEST FRIENDS WILL BE JOINING THE RANKS OF HIGH SCHOOLERS. HE TAKES IN THE MOMENT AS HIS MIND GIVES WAY TO THOUGHTS ABOUT A SONG HE HEARD FOR THE FIRST TIME THAT MORNING.

"HEY, *GUYS,* YOU HEAR THAT NEW *PHIL COLLINS* SONG THEY PLAYED ON THE *RADIO* THIS MORNING?" BILLY ASKS.

THE GUYS LOOK AT HIM WITH BLANK STARES.

"IT WAS *PRETTY GOOD,*" BILLY STARTS. "IT'S ALL ABOUT APPRECIATING WHAT YOU *HAVE,* AND NOT TAKING THOSE THINGS FOR *GRANTED--*"

"--BECAUSE, THERE ARE *PEOPLE OUT THERE* WHO HAVE IT *WAY WORSE* THAN YOU DO." BILLY GOES ON. "I THINK THE SONG WAS CALLED *'ANOTHER DAY IN PARADISE'* OR SOMETHING LIKE THAT."

"YOU KNOW WHAT *WOULD* BE PARADISE?" MIKE ASKS RHETORICALLY. "IS IF YOU GOT THAT *HOLE DUG UP* SO WE CAN GET THAT FIRE GOING!"

"HEH, *YEAH!*" PETE AGREES.

"I DON'T SEE *YOU TWO* DOING ANYTHING TO HELP." BILLY REPLIES. "*WHY* DON'T YOU GO AND FIND SOME *WOOD* FOR THE--"

THE SHOVEL HITS SOMETHING HOLLOW.

"WHAT WAS *THAT?!*" ASKS MIKE.

"*DUNNO.* I HIT SOMETHING..." BILLY REPLIES.

"A *ROCK?* MAYBE *SANDSTONE?*"

"NO, IT WAS *HOLLOW* SOUNDING, LIKE A *BOX* OR SOMETHING"

"MAYBE IT'S *RICH STUFF!!* LIKE *GOONIES!*" PETE SAYS, EXCITED.

"*WHATEVER* IT IS, LET'S DIG IT UP AND *FIND OUT...* "

THE BOYS DIG FOR A FEW MINUTES, THEN FINALLY GET TO THE SURFACE OF WHATEVER IT IS THAT'S IN THE HOLE.

"*WHOA.* WHAT *IS* IT?" PETE SAYS, FULLY INTERESTED .

"LET'S WIPE OFF THE REST OF THE DIRT, AND *FIND OUT.*" BILLY SAYS JUST AS EXCITED. "UH... IT LOOKS LIKE--"

"--IT LOOKS LIKE A *TRUNK* OF SOME SORT." BILLY SAYS WITH CONFIDENCE. "BUT, WHY WOULD SOMEONE BURY THIS OUT *HERE?*"

"*DUDE!* IT *IS* RICH STUFF! *HAS* TO BE! SOMEONE CAME OUT HERE AND BURIED THEIR TREASURE AND *WE FOUND IT!!*" PETE DECLARES.

"WELL, THERES ONLY *ONE WAY* TO FIND OUT... "

1933

A YOUNG COUPLE STANDS IN THE RAIN HOLDING THE TRUNK.

"*AWRIGHT*, WHAT YA GOT FUH MEH *DEN?*" A BALD MAN STANDS BEFORE THE YOUNG COUPLE.

"*WELP*, WHAT AH YA WAITIN' FUH DEN? *OPEN ET UP* SO I KIN *SEE ET!*"

"*SIR*, WE WILL SHOW YOU WHAT'S INSIDE, BUT FIRST, I WANT YOU TO UNDERSTAND HOW *IMPORTANT* THIS MOMENT IS, HOW *SPECIAL* THIS TRUNK AND ITS *CONTENTS* ARE..." THE WOMAN SAYS AS SHE AND HER HUSBAND CLUTCH THE TRUNK WITH FRAIL HANDS.

"*EF* ET'S SO *EMPORTANT*, WHY YOU GITTIN' RID OF ET *DEN?*" THE BALD MAN ASKS.

"BECAUSE *GOD* TOLD US TO BRING IT HERE, *TO YOU.*" THE WOMAN REPLIES.

"HEH, *FECKIN' GAWD*, YA SAY?" THE BALD MAN ROLLS HIS EYES. "*WELP*, LET'S HAVE A LOOK NOW *DEN*."

JUST THEN, THE RAIN STOPS.

AS THE TRUNK OPENS, THE BALD MAN LEANS IN FOR A CLOSER LOOK.

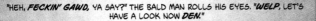

THE BALD MAN GASPS.

"*WHAT* THE *FECK* IS ET?!"

"HE'S NOT AN *'IT'*, HE'S A *HIM*." THE WOMAN REPLIES. "HE'S OUR *SON*, AND WE ARE HERE TO SELL *HIM* TO YOU."

"*EM. ET*. DON'T MATTER." THE BALD MAN SAYS COARSELY. "HOW MUCH YA ASKIN' FOR ET...(COUGH)...*EM?*"

1989

"--IT LOOKS LIKE A *TRUNK* OF SOME SORT." BILLY SAYS WITH CONFIDENCE. "BUT, WHY WOULD SOMEONE BURY THIS OUT *HERE?*"

"*DUDE!* IT *IS* RICH STUFF! *HAS* TO BE! SOMEONE CAME OUT HERE AND BURIED THEIR TREASURE AND *WE FOUND IT!!*" PETE DECLARES.

"WELL, THERES ONLY *ONE WAY* TO FIND OUT... "

BILLY SLOWLY OPENS THE TRUNK. MIKE AND PETE COME AROUND FOR A CLOSER LOOK INSIDE.

"*JACKPOT!*" PETE EXCLAIMS.

"LET'S NOT COUNT OUR CHICKENS *JUST YET.*" BILLY CAUTIONS.

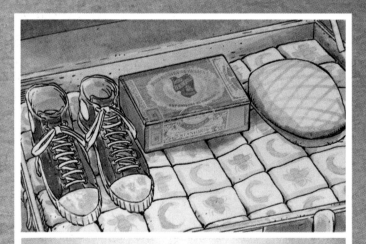

"IT JUST LOOKS LIKE SOMEBODY'S *STUFF.*" BILLY SAYS, A LITTLE DEFLATED.

"*NAH, MAN.* IF IT WAS JUST '*STUFF*', IT WOULDN'T BE LAID OUT ALL *NEAT* LIKE THAT," SAYS MIKE. "THIS LOOKS *DELIBERATE*; ALMOST *CEREMONIAL.*"

"GUYS, THIS *SUCKS.*" PETE ADDS.

"*WELL,* LET'S CHECK IT OUT!--" SAYS BILLY.

"LOOKS LIKE WE'VE GOT A *PAIR OF SHOES...*" BILLY SAYS, DOING INVENTORY.

"*CHUCKS?*" MIKE ASKS.

"ODDLY, *NO.* THESE ARE CALLED '*ONITSUKA TIGERS*' OR SOMETHING." BILLY ANSWERS. "I'VE NEVER HEARD OF THESE BEFORE. *COOL LOOKING.*"

"WHAT *ELSE* IS IN THERE MAN?!" PETE ASKS, IMPATIENTLY. "I *GOTTA* KNOW."

"WELL, THERE'S THIS *CIGAR BOX*..." BILLY SAYS AS HE LIFTS IT OUT OF THE TRUNK. "...AND IT FEELS LIKE THERE'S A BUNCH OF *STUFF* IN IT."

"THAT'S WHAT I'M TALKING ABOUT, DUDE!" PETE DECLARES. "*RICH. STUFF.*"

"FINGERS CROSSED FOR *WAR BONDS,* DUDE." MIKE SAYS. "THOSE ARE WORTH SOME CABBAGE, *FOR SURE.*"

"*OH DAMN!* THERE'S SOME REALLY COOL *SHIT* IN HERE!" BILLY SAYS AS HE OPENS THE CIGAR BOX. "YOU *GOTTA* CHECK THIS OUT~~"

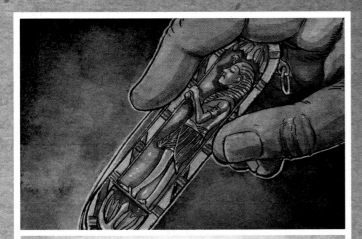

"LOOK AT THIS *POCKET KNIFE!* IT LOOKS LIKE IT'S FROM *ANCIENT EGYPT!*" BILLY SAYS EXCITEDLY.

"I DUNNO, MAN. I DON'T THINK THEY HAD POCKET KNIVES IN ANCIENT EGYPT." MIKE CONTENDS.

"WELL, *WHEREVER* IT CAME FROM, IT'S *COOL.* IT'S GOT *KING TUT* ON IT!" BILLY SAYS.

1933

"*TWENTY-ONE DOLLARS* AND A *BAG OF SUGAR. FECK,* THAT WAS *EASY,*" SAYS THE BALD MAN. "ET'S MAMA WAS *QUITE* THE *DEAL MAKER.* WONDER WHERE SHE LEARNT *THAT* DEN. HEH!"

THE BALD MAN AND THE SKINNY CLOWN MAKE THEIR WAY THROUGH THE CIRCUS GATES WITH THEIR NEWLY ACQUIRED PRIZE.

THE BALD MAN'S NAME IS *LEON SCHECKLE*. HE WAS BORN BEFORE THE TIME OF THE AUTOMOBILE. IN HIS 53 YEARS, HE'S SEEN AND DONE ABOUT ALL THAT LIFE HAS TO OFFER: GOOD AND BAD. NOBODY CALLS HIM BY HIS BIRTH NAME. INSTEAD THEY CALL HIM *"SLIM"* OR *"BOSS"*.

THERE IS A HUSH AS SLIM AND THE SKINNY CLOWN MAKE THEIR WAY DOWN THE CIRCUS ALLEY.

IT'S A RARE THING TO SEE SLIM PART WITH A DIME, LET ALONE TWENTY-ONE DOLLARS. EVEN THE ROUSTABOUTS CAN'T HELP BUT STOP THEIR TASKS TO SEE WHAT IT IS THAT HAS SLIM SPENDING MONEY.

LIKE THE PIED PIPER, SLIM HAS HIS WHOLE CREW UNDER HIS SPELL.

EVEN THE *HEADLINERS* STOP TO TAKE NOTICE.

AS SLIM MAKES HIS WAY TO HIS CARAVAN, HE'S STOPPED BY *COOPER*, THE *CIRCUS GEEK*. COOPER'S CLAIM TO FAME IS THAT HE'LL EAT *ANYTHING* AND CAN TAKE *ANY* KIND OF BEATING YOU GIVE HIM. (MORE ABOUT HIM LATER.)

"UH, *BOSS?*" COOPER ASKS SLIM.

"CAN'T YA *SEE* AHM BIZZY, *COOP?*" SLIM REPLIES.

"WELL, BOSS... I'M WONDERIN' *WHAT'S* IN THAT *TRUNK*, RIGHT THERE?"

SLIM PAUSES FOR A MOMENT, RESOLVES HIMSELF AND SIGHS. "WELL, *FECK* ET."

SLIM SETS DOWN THE TRUNK AND TURNS TO ADDRESS THE SURROUNDING TROUPE. *"AWRIGHT* EVERYBODY, LISTEN UP! AH KIN FEEL YA *FECKIN' STARES* ON DA BACK OF MAH HEAD AND AH WANT *DAT SHIT TA STOP!* SO WHAT AHM GONNA DO, IS SHOW YA WHAT YA WANT TA SEE: WHAT'S IN *THIS HERE TRUNK--"*

"--WELP, ET'S OUR *FUTURE,"* SLIM CONTINUES. "THINGS HAVEN'T BEEN *GREAT* FOR US THIS *PAST SEASON.* WHAT'S IN THIS *TRUNK* IS GONNA *CHANGE* DAT. *SLINK,* HAND ME OUR *FUTURE,* DEN, WOULD YA?"

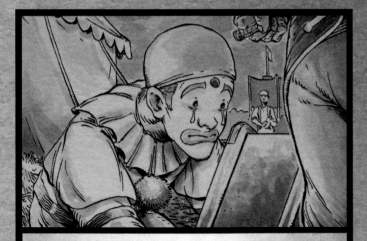

SLINK, THE SKINNY CLOWN. ONE OF THE MOST POPULAR CLOWNS IN THE WHOLE CIRCUS TROUPE. HIS DRAW IS THAT HE HAS THE BEST SLAPSTICK ANTICS EAST OF THE MISSISSIPPI. NOBODY KNOWS HIS REAL NAME. IT'S NOT THAT HE HASN'T TOLD ANYBODY, IT'S THAT NO ONE HAS EVER HEARD HIM SPEAK . EVER.
NOT EVEN ONCE.

SLINK OPENS THE TRUNK AND CAREFULLY REACHES IN.

A RUSH OF GASPS AND COOS COME FROM THE CROWD AS SLINK LIFTS THE HAIR-COVERED BABY FROM OUT OF THE TRUNK.

SLIM TAKES THE BABY FROM SLINK AND HOLDS IT UP TOWARDS THE TROUPE. *"BEHOLD!"* SLIM PROCLAIMS. *"OUR FUTURE! THIS CIRCUS ES MOVIN' ON TA DA NEXT STAGE AND THIS LITTLE FREAK IS OUR TICKET."*

"TAKE A *GOOD LOOK* AT ET!" SLIM CONTINUES. *"THIS ES OUR NEWEST ATTRACTION. AH CALL ET 'DA WOLF BOY'. NO MORE BLANKAROOS FOR US. OUR LITTLE SHOW ES FINALLY GONNA BE ABLE TA COMPETE WITH DEM SOGNO BROS. DEY WONT KNOW WHAT HIT EM! BEST TWENTY-ONE BUCKS AH EVAH SPENT! HEH."*

"TWENTY-ONE DOLLARS?!" THE MYSTIC ASKS, ANNOYED. "WE'RE *THIRTY-TWO* DOLLARS SHORT OF OUR *NUT*, AND YOU'RE *SPENDING* MONEY?!! I THINK I CAN SPEAK FOR THE REST OF THE GROUP WHEN I SAY WE'D LIKE TO *LEAVE* THIS *GOD-FORSAKEN* TOWN!!"

"AIN'T YA NEVAH HEARD OF A BANKSHOT?!" SNAPS SLIM. " 'SIDES, AH USED MAH *OWN* GAWDDAMN *MONEY*, NOT THE CIRCUS'. WAY AH SEE ET, *AHM* DOIN' ALLUH *YA* A FAVOR! YAH DON'T LIKE *ET*, YA KIN GO AN' *FECK* YA SELVES!!"

"*NOW*, EF YA *DON'T MIND*," SLIM CONTINUES. "AHM GONNA GO GIT THIS *THING* SHOW-READY."

"*WAIT, SLIM!!*" SAYS THE FAT LADY, IN AN ACCENT THAT SOUNDS VAGUELY FRENCH. "*WHO* WILL BE TAKING *CARE* OF HIM? WHO WILL *FEED* HIM? *CHANGE* HIM? *WASH* HIM--?"

"*WHY*, MILLIE?" SLIM ASKS, ALREADY KNOWING HER ANSWER. "YOU *VOLUNTEERIN'*?"

"*OUI! S'IL VOUS PLAIT.*" MILLIE REPLIES, WITH A SLIGHT HINT OF DESPERATION IN HER VOICE.

MILLIE DOUBOIR: THE STORY GOES THAT SHE WAS A FAMOUS CABARET DANCER IN PARIS BEFORE SHE JOINED THE CIRCUS. HOW SHE CAME TO BE THE FAT LADY IS A WHOLE OTHER STORY FOR ANOTHER TIME. TODAY THOUGH, ONE OF HER GREATEST WISHES IS ABOUT TO COME TRUE, BUT NOT WITHOUT A COST.

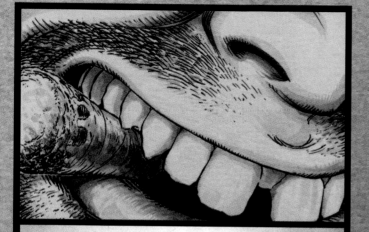

SLIM SMILES A PREDATORY GRIN. HE KNOWS HE HAS HER.

"YA WANT *ET* DEN, MILLIE?" SLIM ASKS, WITH FALSE SINCERITY. "WHAT YA GONNA *DO* FOR ET, DEN?"

"*BECAUSE*, AH WAS JEST GONNA *HAND ET* OVER TO *OL' CYRUS* HERE." SLIM CONTINUES. "HE CAN KEEP *ET* WITH ALL DA *OTHER* ANIMALS. WHATCHA *THINK*, CYRUS?"

"NOW, *SLIM*, I DON'T THINK THAT'S A *GOOD* IDEA." CYRUS REPLIES. "I'M NOT VERSED IN *CHILD* REARING. *BESIDES*--"

"--MY *CATS* WOULD MAKE *MINCED MEAT* OF HIM." CYRUS PROTESTS. "AS MUCH AS I'D *TRY* TO KEEP HIM SAFE, YOU'D *PROBABLY* LOSE OUT ON YOUR *INVESTMENT.* I'M SURE YOU DON'T WANT *THAT.*"

"*C'MON, OL' CYRUS*, AHM SURE YA WOULDN'T LET THINGS GIT *OUTA HAND...*" SLIM SAYS WITH A DEVILISH GRIN. "*HEH!* ...OR, *WOULD* YA?"

SLIM WASN'T JUST TRYING TO BE FUNNY: HE WAS PUTTING CYRUS IN HIS PLACE. SEE, OLD CYRUS HAS ONLY ONE HAND; HIS LEFT HAND. THE OTHER, HE LOST SOME YEARS BACK IT'S NOT SOMETHING THE LION TAMER LIKES TO TALK ABOUT, WHICH IS EXACTLY WHY SLIM CHOSE THE WORDS HE DID.

"*C'MON*, OL' CYRUS, AHM JEST *FECKIN'* WITH *YA!*" SLIM CHUCKLES "*BESIDES,* ET WAS A *RHETORICAL* QUESTION. WHAT *AHM* 'BOUT TA *DO* IS MAKE A *DEAL* WITH MILLIE HERE! *SHE* ACTUALLY WANTS TO TAKE CARE OF *ET!*"

"SO HOW 'BOUT ET *DEN*... YA READY FOR SOME *RESPONSIBILITY*, MILLIE?" SLIM ASKS, AS HE STEPS TOWARD THE FAT LADY.

"OUI, *OUI!* HAND *HIM* TO *ME!*" MILLIE SAYS, EXCITED.

"*AWRIGHT*, DEN!" SAYS SLIM, EYEBROWS RAISED. "*FIRST*, LET'S TALK *TERMS*..."

"*ANYTHING*, SLIM..." MILLIE REPLIES DESPERATELY.

"*WHELP*, AHM GONNA NEED YA TO GET *FATTER!*" SLIM SNAPS. "*LOTS* FATTER."

FATTER.

THAT'S THE LAST THING MILLIE WANTS TO HEAR.

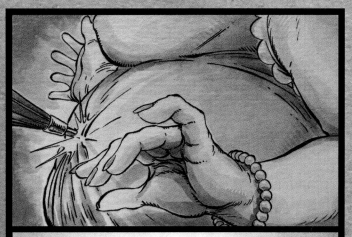

"*THAT'S RIGHT!*" SLIM SPITS. "YA GOTTA GIT BACK TO YA *RECORD* WEIGHT!"

"YA AIN'T AS *FAT* AS YA *USTA* BE," SLIM JABS MILLIE IN THE STOMACH WITH HIS UMBRELLA. "AND IT'S STARTIN' TA *SHOW*--IN THE *NIGHTLY RECEIPTS!* SO *HERE'S* HOW THIS IS GONNA WORK--"

"--COME CHOW TIME, YA *EAT* WHAT YA *GIVEN*," SLIM JABS MILLIE AGAIN. "DEN *AFTAH* THAT, A HELPIN' OF *DA SLOP!* EVERYDAY! *EVERY. MEAL.* ON TOP A *THAT*--"

"--YA GOTTA GIT ON A SCALE AND *WEIGH IN* WHENEVAH *AH SAY!*" SLIM CONTINUES. "AND *EF* YA DROP AS MUCH AS AN *OUNCE*--"

"*ENOUGH!*" SHOUTS CYRUS, IN MILLIE'S DEFENSE.

"SHE'S HAD *ENOUGH*, SLIM." SAYS CYRUS. "WE'RE *ALL* RESPONSIBLE FOR *EARNING*. WHY ARE YOU PICKING ON *HER?* C'MON, CUT HER SOME SLACK."

"NO..." SAYS MILLIE, IN A HUSHED TONE.

"NO. I'LL DO IT." SAYS MILLIE. "I ACCEPT SLIM'S TERMS."

A SAD HUSH FALLS OVER THE TROUPE.

"WELL, *DEN*," SLIM SAYS, SMUGLY. "LOOKS LIKE WE GOT OURSELVES A *DEAL!*"

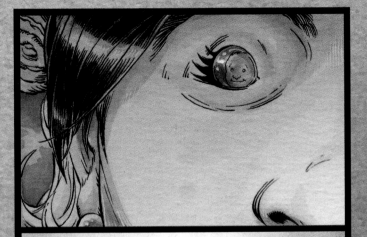

"*THANK YOU*, SLIM." MILLIE SAYS. "*MERCI BEAUCOUP*."

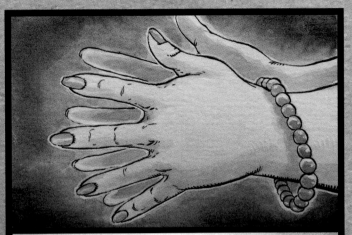

"MAY I HAVE HIM *NOW?* S'IL VOUS PLAIT?" MILLIE ASKS WITH ANTICIPATION.

"NOW, *NOW,* MILLIE," SLIM SAYS, WITH CONDESCENSION. "NOT JUST *YET--*"

"--AH STILL GOTTA GET ET *SHOW-READY*." SLIM SAYS AS HE PATS THE INFANT ON THE HEAD.

"*NOW*, EF YA *ALL* CAN GET BACK TA FECKIN' *WORK*, THAT'D BE GREAT!" SLIM SAYS AS HE MAKES HIS WAY TOWARDS HIS CARAVAN.

"OH, AND *SLINK*, GIVE THAT *TRUNK* TO MILLIE, *WOULD YA?*" SLIM CONTINUES. " '*DA WOLF BOY*' NEEDS SOMEWHERE TO *SLEEP!* "

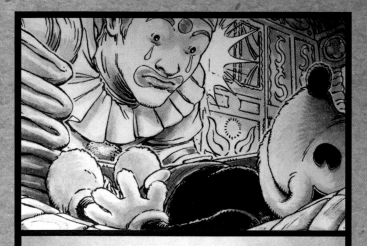

"*ONE MORE THING*, SLINK: GET RID OF THAT FECKIN' *MICKEY MOUSE* TOY. I DON'T WANT DA WOLF BOY THINKIN' ET'S HERE TO *PLAY*. ET'S GOTTA *EARN* THAT PRIVILEGE." SLIM SLAMS THE DOOR ON HIS CARAVAN AS HE GOES INSIDE.

"NOW DEN, *LITTLE MAN*." SLIM SAYS IN AN INFANTILE VOICE. "LET'S GET YOU NICE AND READY FOR THE *SHOW*. YOU'RE GONNA MAKE ME *LOTS* OF MONEY, AREN'T YOU? *YA THIRSTY?* LEMME GET SOMETHIN' TA DRINK."

"*WADDAYA THINK?* YOU THINK YOU CAN BE A GOOD BOY AND *EARN* A SWIG OF THIS *POP?*" SLIM CONTINUES. "AH THINK YA CAN. EN *FACT,* LET'S FIND THAT *BOTTLE OPENER--*"

SLIM REACHES INTO A NEARBY DRAWER.

"AH, YES. HERE ET *ES.*" SLIM FINDS WHAT HE'S LOOKING FOR. "*NOW,* LET'S GET THIS *BOTTLE* OPEN. BUT *FIRST,* THE *EARNING* PART--"

"--GOTTA GET YA *SHOW-READY...*" SLIM FLICKS OUT THE BLADE ON HIS POCKET KNIFE. "...GET YOU *PERFECT.*"

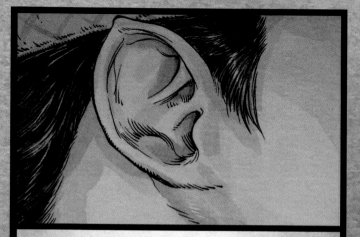

1950

"HOW DID THEY GET THAT WAY?" THE GIRL ASKS IN A SWEET TONE.

"I'M NOT SURE. HAPPENED BEFORE I CAN REMEMBER. THEY'VE JUST *ALWAYS* BEEN THIS WAY, I GUESS." EMMETT REPLIES.

"CAN I TOUCH THEM?" THE GIRL ASKS.

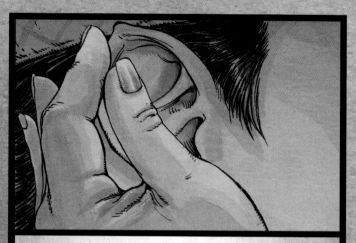

"*SURE.*" EMMETT REPLIES.

"*WOW,* YOUR SKIN IS *REALLY* SOFT. ARE YOU *SURE* YOU'RE NOT A VAMPIRE?" THE GIRL JOKES.

"HEH, *YEAH.* I'M PRETTY *SURE*--" EMMETT REPLIES THROUGH A FANGED GRIN.

"*HEY,* I'M JUST *ASKING.*" THE GIRL CHUCKLES BACK. "*I MEAN,* THE *WHOLE TOWN* HAS BEEN TALKING ABOUT YOU; *'THE BAT BOY'*--"

"ORDER UP--!!"

"BURGER, *WELL DONE.* GARLIC FRIES. *EXTRA GARLIC!*" THE WAITER SETS THE PLATE DOWN.

"AND FOR *YOU*," THE WAITER CONTINUES. "*GRILLED CHEESE* WITH FRIES."

"THANK YOU, SIR." EMMETT REPLIES.

EMMETT TURNS BACK TO THE GIRL. "*EXTRA* GARLIC? NOT JUST GARLIC ON YOUR FRIES, BUT *EXTRA?*"

"HEY, A GIRL CAN'T BE *TOO SURE*--"

THE GIRL'S NAME IS SHELLY MEYERS. THIS IS HER FIRST DATE WITH EMMETT.

"THE ONLY THING YOU CAN BE *SURE* OF WITH *GARLIC,* IS *BAD BREATH!*"

"WELL, MAYBE I'LL HAVE BAD BREATH, BUT I *WON'T* BE ALONE. *YOU'LL* HAVE BAD BREATH *TOO.*"

"OH, *YEAH?* HOW SO?" EMMETT ASKS.

"BECAUSE YOU'RE *SHARING* THEM WITH ME." SHELLY SAYS. *"HERE,* TAKE A *BITE."*

AS SHELLY PUTS THE GARLIC FRY IN EMMETT'S MOUTH, A GROUP OF BOYS FROM SHELLY'S SCHOOL WALK BY THE WINDOW OF THE DINER.

THE GROUP STOPS TO WATCH WHAT'S GOING ON INSIDE. THE SCENE DOESN'T SIT WELL WITH ONE OF THE BOYS IN PARTICULAR.

HIS NAME IS TOMMY MEYERS. HE'S THE CAPTAIN OF THE ASHLAND HIGH SCHOOL FOOTBALL TEAM, AND SHELLY MEYERS IS HIS TWIN SISTER. AT THIS MOMENT, HE'S CONTEMPLATING THE SMARTEST PLAY FOR THE SITUATION AT HAND.

SHOULD HE GO INSIDE AND MAKE A SCENE? OR SHOULD HE WAIT IT OUT; LET THINGS GO?

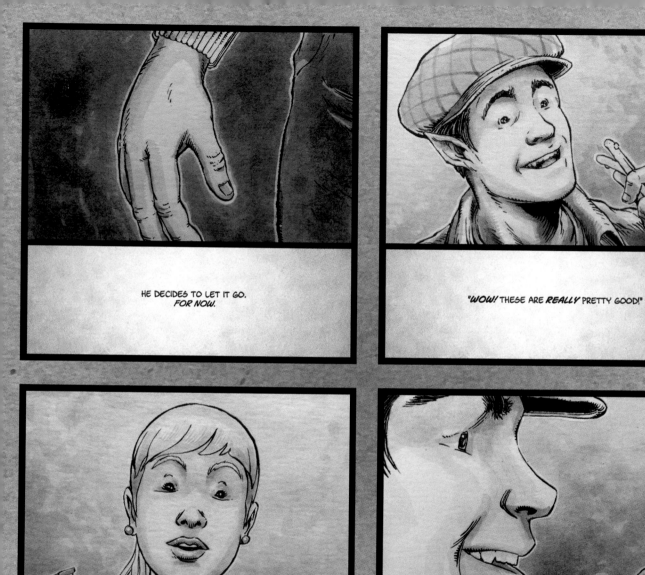

HE DECIDES TO LET IT GO.
FOR NOW.

"WOW! THESE ARE *REALLY* PRETTY GOOD!"

SHELLY STARES AT EMMETT AS IF SOMETHING IS GOING TO HAPPEN.

"WHAT?" EMMETT ASKS, SMILING. "DID YOU THINK I WAS GOING TO BURST
INTO A *BALL OF FLAMES?"*

"NO, I JUST WASN'T *100% SURE* THAT YOU WEREN'T *REALLY* A VAMPIRE." SHELLY SAYS. "ONE THING IS FOR SURE THOUGH: *YOU'VE GOT BAD BREATH!*"

"MAY I SUGGEST YOU WASH DOWN THOSE FRIES WITH SOME *TASTY POP?*" SHELLY OFFERS.

"UM, THANKS." EMMETT REPLIES. "BUT I DON'T DRINK THAT STUFF. NEVER REALLY LIKED IT. EVEN THE *SMELL* MAKES MY STOMACH TURN."

"BUT, I'D BE *GLAD* TO OPEN IT FOR YOU!" EMMETT SAYS WITH A CHUCKLE.

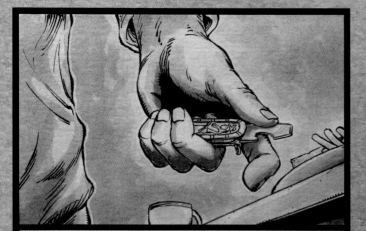

EMMETT FLICKS A BLADE OPEN ON HIS POCKET KNIFE.

PFFFZZZZZZTT!

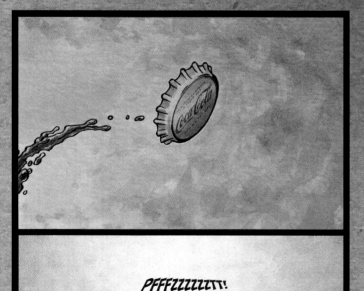

PFFFZZZZZZTT!

1989

TINK TINK *TINK*

"YEAH BUDDY! THIS POCKET KNIFE IS *CHAMPION* AT OPENING BOTTLES!"
PETE SAYS WITH DELIGHT.

"COLD *SUDS* WITH THE *BUDS*..." SAYS PETE. "*THAT'S* WHAT IT'S ALL ABOUT. *AM I RIGHT?!*"

"MAN, *YOU SAID IT!*" SAYS BILLY. "SO *THAT'S* WHAT YOU WERE UP TO AT *CASE'S.* NICELY DONE, MAN!"

"HEH, *YOU KNOW IT!* NOW BOTTOMS UP, GENTS, WHILE THEY'RE STILL *COLD.*" SAYS PETE, AS HE TAKES A SWIG.

"I DUNNO. MAYBE IT'S THE *BEER* TALKING, BUT, THIS KNIFE HAS GIVEN ME A CRAZY IDEA." PETE SAYS. "*WHAT IF--*"

"--WHAT IF THERE WAS A *COMIC* THAT TELLS THE HISTORY OF RANDOM ITEMS? LIKE THIS *KNIFE,* OR A *PIMP CANE* FOR EXAMPLE. YOU COULD CALL IT '*PAWN*' AS IN *PAWN SHOP,* AND EACH ISSUE STARTS THE SAME BY SHOWING A DIFFERENT PAWN SHOP. WE'D GO INSIDE AND FIND THE ITEM, THEN FLASH BACK AND TELL THE *HISTORY* OF IT." PETE CONTINUES. "THINK OF HOW *COOL* IT WOULD BE. YOU COULD TELL THE HISTORY OF, SAY, *AN ENGAGEMENT RING.* IT COULD BE A *TRAGEDY.* OR A *SAMURAI SWORD...* GO TO JAPAN. THE POSSIBILITIES ARE *ENDLESS!*"

"I WAS THINKING THE *SAME THING*--" SAYS BILLY. "WELL, *SORTA* THE SAME, BUT NOT AS A *COMIC*. I WAS WONDERING WHAT THE STORY IS BEHIND THE *STUFF* IN THIS *CIGAR BOX*." BILLY TAKES A LONG LOOK AT THE BOX'S CONTENTS. "YOU'RE RIGHT ABOUT ONE THING: *THE POSSIBILITIES ARE ENDLESS*."

"I MEAN, TAKE THIS *POCKET WATCH* FOR EXAMPLE--" SAYS BILLY. "I BET THAT EVEN *ONE DAY* IN ITS HISTORY WOULD BE COOL TO KNOW ABOUT."

1938

"*GODDAMNIT!* WHERE IS *HE?*" A VOICE BOOMS. "THE SHOW IS RUNNING *FIVE MINUTES* LATE!!"

THIS IS *EARL HASTINGS*. HE'S THE CIRCUS' BARKER AND ALSO THE GUY WHO MAKES SURE THINGS RUN ON TIME. TODAY, THINGS ARE NOT GOING HIS WAY.

"HAS *ANYBODY* SEEN THE *KID?*" EARL ASKS IN A COMMANDING TONE. "IF HE'S NOT ON STAGE *PRONTO*, HEADS ARE GONNA ROLL!!"

"*HEY, EARL--*" A WORKER RUNS UP IN HASTE. "*--SLIM* IS LOOKIN' FOR YOU, AND HE'S *PISSED.* PEOPLE ARE *COMPLAININ'!*"

"*MOTHER FUCKER!* WHERE IS THAT *KID?!*" EARL REPLIES. "WHERE'S SLIM RIGHT NOW?"

"HE'S IN THE *BIG TENT.* MAYBE IT'S BETTER YOU GO AN' SEE HIM?" THE WORKER SAYS WITH CONCERN.

AMIDST THE CHAOS, NEITHER MAN NOTICES THE MEN INSIDE *THIS* TENT, WHO ARE THERE TO KEEP AN EYE ON SLIM'S CIRCUS....

"*YEAH,* YOU'RE PROBABLY *RIGHT,*" EARL SAYS, STEPPING DOWN FROM THE BARKER STAND. "LET'S JUST GET IT *OVER* WITH--"

"EARL! *EARL!* WE *FOUND* HIM!" A VOICE YELLS FROM BEHIND. "WE FOUND THE *KID!!*"

"WE FOUND THE KID, EARL, AND *IT AIN'T GOOD!*" THE OTHER WORKER GRABS EARL AND PULLS HIM AWAY IN A HURRY.

"OVER *HERE!* OVER *HERE!!*" THE WORKER HASTENS EARL. "*THERE,* IN CAGE *FIVE!*"

"SWEET JESUS... *NO!*" EARL STOPS DEAD AT CAGE FIVE.

"*CYRUS!!* SOMBODY *GET CYRUS!!*" EARL YELLS IN A PANIC. "HOW THE *HELL* DID THE KID GET IN *THERE?!*"

"*EARL.* LOOK! *THE ROOF!!*" THE WORKER YELLS. "THE KID MUSTA BROKE THROUGH *THERE.*"

"HOW THE *HELL* ARE WE GONNA GET IN THERE?" EARL SAYS, FRUSTRATED. "THIS GODDAMN *PAD LOCK*... WILL *SOMEBODY* TELL ME WHERE *CYRUS* IS?! IF WE DON'T GET IN THERE *SOON,* THAT KID'S AS GOOD AS *DEAD*... IF HE ISN'T ALREADY."

EARL TURNS TOWARD THE TIGER. "C'MON, *BIG KITTY,* BACK *AWAY* FROM THE *KID--*"

"*--C'MON* KITTY..." EARL PLEADS.

THE BIG CAT ROARS AT EARL. THE TIGER'S NAME IS *BOSEPH.* HE'S BEEN WITH THE CIRCUS FOR EXACTLY THIRTEEN DAYS.

THIRTEEN.

SOME SAY THE NUMBER IS BAD LUCK.

"*OH,* NO! *BOSEPH!!*" CYRUS SAYS MORTIFIED AS HE ENTERS THE SCENE. "*LET ME THROUGH!!* I'VE GOT THE *KEYS* RIGHT *HERE!!*"

"WHERE THE *HELL* WERE YOU, *CYRUS?*" EARL ASKS, LAYING FAULT ON CYRUS.

"I WAS HELPING *MILLIE* BACK TO HER TRAILER LIKE I *ALWAYS DO!*" CYRUS REPLIES AS HE FUMBLES WITH THE KEYS. "LET'S PLAY THE *BLAME GAME* SOME OTHER TIME..."

"THE *BLAME GAME?* IT'S YOUR FUCKING *TIGER* THAT'S IN THERE WITH THAT *KID.*"

"LET ME GET THIS **STRAIGHT**--" CYRUS PAUSES. "IT'S **MY** FAULT THAT THE **KID**, WHO IS ON **YOUR** WATCH, IS IN THERE WITH MY **TIGER**, IN **ITS** CAGE, WHERE IT **BELONGS?** THAT'S WHAT YOU'RE SAYING?"

EARL DOESN'T HAVE A REPLY.

"**MORON.**" CYRUS CONTINUES. "YOU JUST DON'T WANT TO ANSWER TO **SLIM** FOR THIS."

CYRUS OPENS THE TIGER'S CAGE.

"**WHAT?** STILL NOTHING TO SAY, **EARL?**" CYRUS ASKS WHILE ENTERING THE CAGE. "WELL, **ONE** OF US HAS STILL HAS TO DO OUR **JOB.** LOOKS LIKE THAT'S **ME.** GOOD LUCK WITH **SLIM.**"

EARL FREEZES. CYRUS' WORDS SINK IN. THE ONLY THOUGHT OCCUPYING EARL'S MIND AT THE MOMENT IS HOW TO MAKE IT THROUGH SLIM'S WRATH ONCE HE'S FOUND OUT WHAT'S HAPPENED TO THE KID. EARL HAS TO THINK OF SOMETHING AND FAST.

CYRUS ENTERS THE TIGER'S CAGE AS ONLOOKERS FORM A CROWD.

"**C'MON,** BOSEPH, BE A **GOOD GIRL...**" CYRUS SAYS AS HE INCHES CLOSER TO THE BIG CAT.

EARL WATCHES WITH A HAWK'S GAZE.

WHAT CYRUS SEES NEXT IS UNEXPECTED.

THE KID'S HAND STARTS TO MOVE. CYRUS IS RELIEVED. THE KID'S ALIVE.
SOMETHING IS DIFFERENT THOUGH. SOME OF THE HAIR ON HIS ARM IS MISSING.

BOSEPH EYES CYRUS.

THE TIGER SITS UP. CYRUS LOOSENS HIS GRIP, LETTING THE WHIP UNWIND.
THE TENSION IS THICK.

"WELL, *I'LL BE...* " CYRUS SAYS IN COMPLETE DISBELIEF.

BOSEPH GENTLY LICKS THE KID'S WOUNDS. SMALL PATCHES OF HAIR COME OFF WITH EACH LICK.

CYRUS TURNS TOWARDS EARL. "LOOKS LIKE YOUR *ASS* MAY BE OFF THE HOOK AFTER ALL, *EARL*. THE KID'S *ALIVE*. STILL, SLIM'S *GONNA WONDER* WHY THE SHOW DIDN'T HAPPEN. YOU BETTER COME UP WITH SOMETHING... "

EARL TURNS, HIS MIND RACING WITH THOUGHTS OF HOW TO MINIMIZE THE SITUATION. SLIM WONT LIKE HEARING ABOUT IT, ANY WAY IT'S TOLD. MAKING SLIM HAPPY... THAT'S THE KEY TO EARL MAKING IT OUT OF THIS SITUATION IN ONE PIECE.

"MAKE SLIM HAPPY." EARL THINKS. "ABOUT THE ONLY THING THAT MAKES SLIM HAPPY IS MONEY. SOLVE THAT, AND YOU'RE IN."

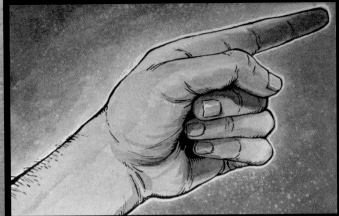

"SWEET BABY JESUS! *LOOK!!!*" SOMEONE CRIES OUT FROM THE CROWD.

CYRUS STEPS OUT OF THE CAGE WITH THE KID, WHO SLOWLY BEGINS TO STIR. THE CROWD STARTS TO CHEER.

CYRUS TURNS BACK TO EARL. "I'M TAKING THE KID TO *MILLIE*--"

"--IT LOOKS LIKE HE'S GOT A *MILD CONCUSSION*." CYRUS CONTINUES.

" *COUGH! COUGH!* I'M REALLY *SORRY*, CYRUS." SAYS THE KID. "I JUST WANTED TO SEE BOSEPH WITHOUT HER *SEEING ME...*"

"*SHHH...*NOW NOW, KID. I'M GONNA TAKE YOU TO YOUR *MAMA*." CYRUS SAYS IN A GENTLE TONE.

CYRUS TURNS AWAY AND WALKS THROUGH THE CROWD.

"WELL *I'LL BE!* I'VE *NEVER* SEEN ANYTHING LIKE IT *BEFORE!*" A MAN SAYS FROM THE CROWD. "SHOOT, I'D EVEN PAY *DOUBLE* TO SEE IT AGAIN. IT WAS LIKE A *SUPER CAT AND DOG SHOW!*"

"A *CAT* AND *DOG* SHOW... " EARL GETS AN IDEA.

MOMENTS LATER IN SLIM'S CARAVAN...

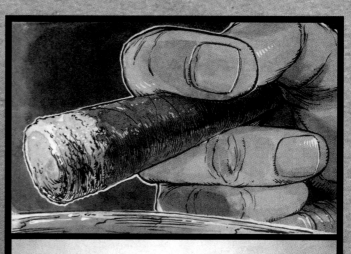

THE TRAILER HAS A MUSTY ODOR AND IS FILLED WITH EVERY SORT OF ODDITY THAT ONE CAN IMAGINE.

"SIT *DOWN*, EARL. TELL ME WHY THE *FECK* THERE WAS NO *DOG SHOW*." SLIM DOESN'T WASTE TIME GETTING TO THE POINT.

"I ASKED FOR YOU TO JOIN US, SO YOU COULD CATCH *DROPPED BALLS--*" SLIM CONTINUES."--NOT, *DROP BALLS.* YOU DROPPED THE *GAME-WINNING* BALL TODAY..."

"...*WORST* OF ALL--" SLIM GOES ON. "--YOU LET THE DOG *GET HURT*."

"*OH*, SO YOU *KNOW*." EARL SAYS, TAKEN ABACK.

"I FECKIN' KNOW *EVERYTHING* THAT HAPPENS IN THIS *GAWDAMN* PLACE." SLIM SAYS GRUFFLY. "THAT'S WHY IT'S CALLED *'SLIM'S BIG SHOWS,'* AND *NOT* FECKIN' *'EARL'S'!*"

"WELL, *SURE*, THE KID *DID* HIT HIS HEAD, *BUT--*" EARL CONTINUES.

"--YOU GOTTA **BREAK** A FEW **EGGS** TO MAKE AN **OMELETTE**," EARL SAYS.

"WHAT THE FECK'S **THAT** SUPPOSED TO MEAN?!" ASKS SLIM.

"WELL, WHERE YOU SEE A **DROPPED BALL**, I SEE **OPPORTUNITY**," SAYS EARL.

"HOW'S THAT **DEN?**" SLIM ASKS, GENUINELY CURIOUS.

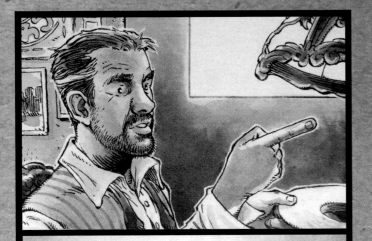

"A **CAT AND DOG SHOW**. JUST LIKE THE ONES IN THE **CARTOONS**, BUT IN **REAL LIFE**," EARL EXPLAINS.

"I DON'T FOLLOW...," SAYS SLIM.

"YOU KNOW HOW I ALWAYS GO INTO TOWN ON MY DAYS OFF?" ASKS EARL. "WELL, IT'S TO GO TO THE **PICTURE SHOW**. BEFORE THE SHOW, THEY PLAY THESE **CARTOONS** WITH A **CAT AND DOG**. THEY ANTAGONIZE EACH OTHER WITH GREAT COMEDIC EFFECT--"

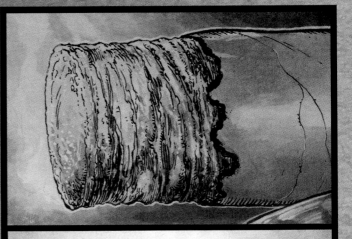

EARL DETAILS HOW A CAT AND DOG SHOW WORKS: ONE STIRS UP THE OTHER, THE OTHER GIVES CHASE, AND A SERIES OF PRATFALLS AND GAGS FOLLOW WITH EITHER THE CAT OR THE DOG ENDING UP WITH THE UPPER HAND. IN THIS CASE, THE DOG (THE KID), WOULD BE THE HERO.

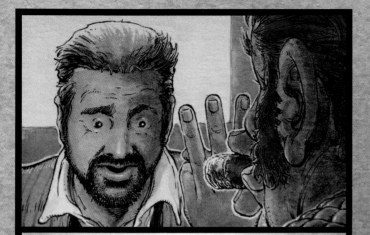

"I'M *TELLING* YOU, SLIM--" EARL GOES ON WITH DESPERATION. "YOU *CAN'T LOSE*. THE CAT AND DOG SHOW WILL PULL IN *THREE TIMES* WHAT THE REGULAR SHOW IS DOING. MAKE IT AN *EVENT!*"

THERE'S A LONG SILENCE BETWEEN THE TWO MEN.

"AWRIGHT *DEN,* EARL." SLIM BREAKS THE QUIET. "YA GOT *TWO WEEKS* TO PROVE IT--"

"--AND IF THIS *CAT AND DOG SHOW* AIN'T UP TO SNUFF--" SLIM CONTINUES. "--I'M TAKING YOUR FECKIN' *EYE.*"

THREE WEEKS LATER

A WORKER OUTSIDE THE TENT LISTENS IN ON CYRUS AND EARL'S CONVERSATION.

"NOW, *EARL,* I'M GONNA TELL YOU THE SAME THING I'VE *BEEN* TELLING YOU FROM THE START--" CYRUS EXPLAINS. "--THE CAT *WONT* CHASE THE KID. THE CAT *WONT* DO *ANYTHING* TO HARM THE KID. *IN FACT,* THE CAT GOES OUT OF HER *WAY* TO MAKE SURE THE KID IS *SAFE.*"

"I MEAN, *LOOK* AT THEM--" CYRUS SAYS WITH SINCERITY.

"--THEY'RE *BEST PALS!*" CYRUS CONTINUES. "LIKE *TWO PEAS* IN A POD."

"YEAH--" EARL SIGHS. "IT'S *CLEAR* TO ME NOW."

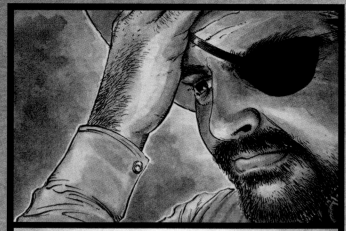

EARL GOES QUIET FOR A MOMENT.

"LOOK, CYRUS. *I FUCKED UP.*" EARL BREAKS THE SILENCE. "I WAS *TRYING* TO BE QUICK ON MY *FEET.* BE THE *GUY* THAT MY REPUTATION *SAYS* I AM. *INSTEAD,* I MADE A *MISTAKE.* A *BIG* MISTAKE."

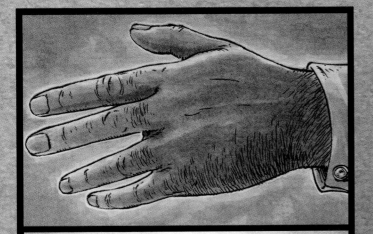

"I GUESS WHAT I'M *TRYING* TO SAY IS, IS THAT I'M *SORRY... REALLY SORRY--*" EARL EXTENDS HIS HAND. "--AND, I *NEED* YOUR HELP."

CYRUS STARES AT EARL'S HAND FOR A MOMENT. HE THINKS ABOUT THE LAST THREE WEEKS AND THE IMPOSSIBLE MISSION THAT EARL TASKED HIM WITH. THEN CYRUS LOOKS AT EARL'S EYE. IT'S THEN HE UNDERSTANDS THAT EARL'S APOLOGY IS GENUINE.

"*ALL RIGHT,* EARL--" CYRUS SAYS.

"--I'LL *HELP* YOU." CYRUS CONTINUES. "MY *ONLY* CONDITION IS, *IF* WE'RE GONNA DO THIS *CAT AND DOG SHOW,* THEN WE'RE GOING TO DO IT *MY WAY.* NO EXCEPTIONS. DO WE HAVE A *DEAL?*"

"*YES.* YES WE DO." EARL REPLIES WITH ENTHUSIASM.

THREE WEEKS LATER

THE SOUND OF UPROARIOUS APPLAUSE FILLS THE AIR.

"OH, WOW! DADDY, I WISH I HAD A *REAL* TIGER! WE SHOULD GET A *REAL TIGER!"* SAYS THE VOICE OF AN EXCITED CHILD.

"NOW, SON, WHAT WOULD WE *FEED* IT? WHERE WOULD WE *KEEP* HIM?" A FATHER'S VOICE REPLIES.

"BUT THESE GUYS, YOU CAN KEEP *ANYWHERE!"* THE FATHER HANDS HIS SON STUFFED VERSIONS OF THE KID AND BOSEPH.

"CAN WE FEED 'EM POPCORN AND *COTTON CANDY?!"* THE SON ASKS ENTHUSIASTICALLY.

"YOU BETCHA, MY BOY." THE FATHER REPLIES.

"YOU'RE THE BEST, DADDY!!" SAYS THE SON.

"GET YOUR DOG AND CAT DOLLS *RIGHT HERE!"* EARL SHOUTS. *"RELIVE THE EXCITEMENT* OF THE *DOG AND CAT SHOW!!"*

"I'LL TAKE A SET, MISTER!!" YELLS AN EXCITED CUSTOMER.

"I'LL TAKE ONE TOO!"   "RIGHT HERE! RIGHT HERE!"

"OVER HERE! I'LL TAKE A SET!"

THE EXCITED CROWD SHOVES THEIR MONEY AT EARL.

"HEY, *BOSS*, SLIM WANTS TO SEE YOU." SAYS A WORKER. "HE'S OVER IN *CLOWN ALLEY* WITH MILLIE AND SLINK."

MINUTES LATER.

"*EARL*, MY BOY!!" SHOUTS SLIM. "WELL, LOOK AT *YOU!* ALL... *PROFITABLE*."

"....*YOU'RE* WELCOME, *EARL*." SAYS SLIM IN AN EXPECTANT TONE.

AN AWKWARD SILENCE FOLLOWS.

"UH...*THANK YOU?*" EARL SAYS, UNSURE.

"YOU SEEM *CONFUSED*. EVER SINCE OUR LAST '*DISCUSSION*' ABOUT YOUR *FAILURES*, YOU'VE SEEMED TO GAIN *FOCUS*." SLIM CONTINUES. "I'VE NOTICED, YOU'VE KEPT YOUR *EYE* ON THE BALL. *IT'S CLEAR*, YOU HAVEN'T *LOST SIGHT* OF YOUR GOALS--"

"--WAY *I* SEE IT, I DID *YOU* A FAVOR," SLIM GOES ON. "*BESIDES*, IT'S A GOOD *STORY*."

" I MEAN, WHAT'S *SPECIAL* ABOUT A SIMPLE *CIRCUS BARKER?*" SLIM CONTINUES. "*NOTHING*. BUT A *ONE-EYED* BARKER, NOW, *THAT'S* REMARKABLE; WORTH *TELLING* A FRIEND. THAT'S WHAT IT'S *ALL* ABOUT: *A STORY--*"

EARL STANDS THERE SILENT AS THE TROUPE OF CLOWNS STARE AND WHISPER.

"--I MEAN, *C'MON, EARL!*" SLIM GOES ON.

"*LOOK* AT MILLIE HERE, DEN." SAYS SLIM. "TWO *MORE* POUNDS AND SHE'S GOT THE *RECORD* FOR FATTEST LADY IN THE *WORLD*. THEM *SOGNO BROTHERS* CAN'T SAY THEY'VE GOT THE FATTEST LADY. *I CAN!* WHY? BECAUSE, *STORY*."

"YOU'RE A FAN OF STORY. AIN'T YOU, *MILLIE?*" SLIM TAUNTS. *"TWO MORE* POUNDS, AND YOUR STORY GETS *BETTER! SLINK,* GIVE HER THE *SLOP!"*

SLINK PUTS A PIE TIN OF CIRCUS SLOP IN FRONT OF MILLIE.

"BOTTOMS UP, BIG GIRL!" SLIM LAUGHS.

SLIM WATCHES WITH SICK DELIGHT AS MILLIE FORCES DOWN THE SLOP.

AT THAT SAME MOMENT, OUTSIDE THE TENT.

"UGH, THAT'S SO *GROSS!--"* A KID EXCLAIMS

COOPER STANDS BEHIND THE GROUP OF KIDS WITH AN UNMISTAKABLE GRIN.

"YOU'LL *EAT* THIS FOR A *NICKEL?"* THE KID ASKS.

"YEAH, KID, BUT A NICKEL *EACH.*" COOPER REPLIES.

"A NICKEL *EACH?!*" ASKS THE KID.

"*YEAH,* KID. THIS AIN'T ME EATING A *BUG,* A *TIN CAN* OR SOME OTHER *TRASH--*" COOPER GOES ON. "THIS IS ME EATING *DOG SHIT.* THE *WHOLE THING.* NOW LET'S SEE THEM *BUFFALOS!*"

"NOW, *HOLD ON* A GODDAMN SECOND!" A VOICE BOOMS OUT.

"A *DOG SHIT?!* HOW DO WE KNOW IT'S NOT *FAKE?*" ASKS A BIG MAN IN A FANCY SUIT. "SEE, ME AND MY KID CAME HERE FOR A *REAL* SHOW. WE SAW THE DOG AND CAT THING. IT WAS LIKE A *CARTOON.* I WANT *REAL.* HOW ABOUT INSTEAD OF *FIFTEEN CENTS* FROM THESE *KIDS,* I PAY YOU A *WHOLE BUCK!* BUT... YOU'VE GOT TO EAT *MY SHIT!*"

"MY DAD'LL *PAY* YOU TOO! HE'S *RICH!!!*" SAYS THE BIG MAN'S SON. "AND *POWERFUL!!*"

"*SURE, SURE...*" SAYS COOPER. "I'LL TAKE YOUR *DEAL,* BUT I GET YOUR *KID'S* NICKEL TOO."

THE MEN AGREE TO THE TERMS AND THE BIG MAN IN THE FANCY SUIT HEADS STRAIGHT FOR THE CLOSEST OUTHOUSE. A HEALTHY AMOUNT OF TIME PASSES AS A CACOPHONOUS ARRAY OF SOUNDS AND SMELLS EMIT FROM THE WOODEN BOX.

THE BIG MAN IN THE FANCY SUIT WALKS OUT OF THE OUTHOUSE WITH A WASH BOWL IN HIS HANDS.

"HEH, HEH. *HOT* TO *ORDER!*" THE BIG MAN SETS THE BOWL IN FRONT OF COOPER.

"--SEEN *WORSE.*" COOPER SAYS THROUGH A WRY SMILE.

"EW, *GROSS!* I THINK I'M GONNA *THROW UP!*"
"AW *HECK* NO!"
"*HA, HA!* YEAH, DADDY, *PEANUTS!*"

"WILL YOU *PLEASE* QUIT YOUR *SQUAWKING?!--*" SAYS COOPER, CUTTING THROUGH THE NOISE.

"--I WANNA DIG INTO THIS!" SAYS COOPER AS HE RAISES HIS SPOON.

COOPER DIGS INTO THE BOWL. THEN...

...COOPER TAKES A BITE.

NO. YOU'RE NOT SEEING THINGS.

COOPER IS.

THIS IS EXACTLY HOW HE CAN DO WHAT HE DOES. HE'S MASTERED THE ART OF DELUSION.

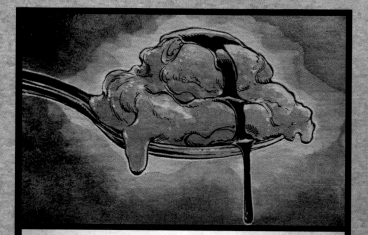

TO COOPER, THIS ISN'T A SPOONFUL OF HUMAN FECES. IT'S A SPOONFUL OF HEAVEN. TRIPLE FUDGE ICE CREAM WITH CHOCOLATE SYRUP ON TOP...

...STENCH-FILLED AIR BECOMES A SUMMER BREEZE. FLIES BECOME BUTTERFLIES. TO ESCAPE, TO "FLY AWAY", COOPER CHANGES THE THINGS HE DOESN'T LIKE INTO THE THINGS HE DOES. THE UNPLEASANT BECOMES THE PLEASANT...

....THE REAL BECOMES THE SURREAL.

"HEYA *KID*, YER DOIN' A *GREAT JOB* EATING THAT *SUNDAE!* SHOW 'EM HOW IT'S *DONE!*" SAYS BUSBY THE SKEETER, COOPER'S LIFELONG PAL.

WHEN THE ABUSE IS SO SATURATED AS IT WAS FOR COOPER, AND AT SUCH AN EARLY AGE, HIS MIND HAS NO LIMITS AS TO WHAT IT CAN CREATE TO COPE WITH THE WORLD AROUND HIM. COOPER TURNED HIS CURSE INTO HIS GIFT.

"YER *DOIN'* IT, KID! YOU'RE ALMOST ACROSS THE *FINISH LINE*. JUST A *FEW* BITES LEFT!" THE SKEETER CONTINUES TO CHAMPION HIS PAL.

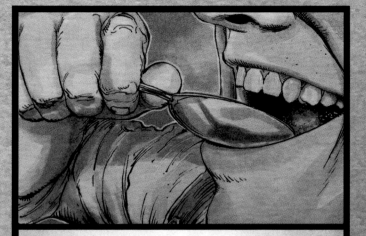

BUSBY'S WORDS OF ENCOURAGEMENT PROPEL COOPER THROUGH THE LAST BITES OF THE CHALLENGE.

AFTER A QUICK TIDYING UP, COOPER TAKES A VICTORIOUS LOOK AT HIS CHALLENGERS.

COOPER SEES HIS AUDIENCE FOR WHAT THEY ARE: A COUPLE OF PIGS, A SCARED PUP, AND A CURIOUS BOOK OWL.

JUST AS QUICKLY AS COOPER CREATES HIS DELUSIONS, HE ALSO MAKES THEM FADE AWAY.

"HOT DAMN, BOY!! NOW THAT... WAS A REAL SHOW!!" EXCLAIMS THE BIG MAN IN A FANCY SUIT.

"YOU EARNED EVERY PENNY OF THIS DOLLAR!"

"DOLLAR, FIVE" SAYS COOPER.

"COME AGAIN?" ASKS THE BIG MAN.

"I SAID I'D TAKE YOUR DOLLAR... AND YOUR KID'S NICKEL... REMEMBER?" COOPER CLARIFIES.

"HA! I GUESS THE APPLE REALLY DOESN'T FALL FAR FROM THE TREE!" LAUGHS THE BIG MAN.

"WHAT'S THAT SUPPOSED TO MEAN?" COOPER ASKS, ALMOST OFFENDED.

"WHAT IT MEANS, COOPER SCHECKLE, IS THAT YOU'RE JUST LIKE YOUR DADDY!" THE BIG MAN CHUCKLES.

COOPER IS PERPLEXED.

"HOW'D YOU KNOW MY PA?" HE ASKS.

"YOU REALLY DON'T REMEMBER ME, COOP?" THE BIG MAN REPLIES. "AND HERE I THOUGHT YOU WERE SHOWING OFF ON PURPOSE..."

"YOU WANTED A *REAL* SHOW. I GAVE YOU A *REAL* SHOW." COOPER EXPLAINS "WHAT'S THIS ALL *ABOUT* ANYWAY?"

"I'M HERE TO SEE YOUR *PA.*" SAYS THE BIG MAN. "KNOW WHERE HE MIGHT BE?"

"HE'S OVER *THERE* IN CLOWN ALLEY. IT'S THE SECOND TENT ON THE RIGHT." COOPER SAYS AS THE BIG MAN WALKS TOWARDS THE TENTS. "*HEY!* WHAT DO YOU WANT WITH MY PA?!"

"FAMILY REUNION... *NEPHEW.*" THE BIG MAN CALLS BACK.

THE BIG MAN'S NAME IS *EDDIE SCHECKLE.* HE'S SLIM'S LITTLE BROTHER. TODAY, EDDIE ISN'T HERE AS SLIM'S BROTHER, BUT AS A REPRESENTATIVE OF *"THE ORGANIZATION."* HE'S HERE TO TELL SLIM THAT HE'S PAST DUE ON PAYING "ROYALTIES."

MEANWHILE, OUTSIDE THE MAIN TENT, CYRUS AND THE KID RELAX AFTER THEIR SOLD-OUT PERFORMANCE.

"YOU DID *GREAT,* KID." SAYS CYRUS. "THE SHOW JUST KEEPS GETTING *BETTER* WITH PERFORMANCE. WHAT DO YOU THINK OF YOUR *DOLLS?* LOOKS *JUST* LIKE YOU, EH?"

"THESE ARE *ME* AND *BOSEPH?*" ASKS THE KID. "OTHER KIDS PLAY PRETEND THEY'RE *ME?*"

"WELL, *YEAH*, KID. THEY SEE THE *SHOW* AND THEY SEE THE KIND OF *FUN* YOU'RE HAVING... I MEAN, WHAT KID *WOULDN'T* WANT A PET TIGER AS HIS BEST PAL?" CYRUS REPLIES.

"BEST *KITTY* PAL." THE KID CORRECTS CYRUS. "*YOU'RE* MY BEST PAL, CYRUS. I WANT TO BE LIKE *YOU*."

"*NO*, YOU *DON'T*." CYRUS SAYS QUICKLY.

"*WHY?* BECAUSE OF YOUR *HAND?*" THE KID ASKS. "*I'M SURE* IT WAS A *MEAN OL' LION* WHO DONE IT."

"YOU KNOW *KID*, THAT'S WHAT *EVERYBODY* THINKS. '*A CAT GOT 'IM!*' I NEVER SAY OTHERWISE." CYRUS TURNS TO THE KID. "*SLIM* SAYS IT ADDS TO MY *STORY*: SOMEONE SEES THE *ONE* MISSING HAND AND THEY WANNA SEE THE SHOW *MORE*. WHY? FOR THEM IT ADDS *TENSION*, LIKE IT'S GONNA HAPPEN *AGAIN*, BUT THERE'S NO '*AGAIN*' SINCE IT WASN'T *A CAT* WHO DONE IT IN THE FIRST PLACE."

"NOT A CAT... " THE KID SAYS TO HIMSELF. "WELL, HOW *DID* YOU LOSE YOUR HAND?"

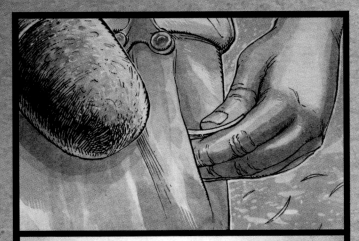

"KID, YOU KNOW THE *DIFFERENCE* BETWEEN *RIGHT* AND *WRONG*, *GOOD* AND *BAD*, DON'T YOU?" CYRUS ASKS.

"I THINK SO." THE KID REPLIES.

"WELL, *SOMETIMES* YOU MAY END UP DOING SOMETHING THAT YOU *THINK* IS RIGHT, BUT AFTER YOU *REALLY* THINK ABOUT IT, YOU DID THE *WRONG* THING FOR THE *WRONG* REASONS." CYRUS CONTINUES. "*THAT*, IN A NUTSHELL, IS WHAT HAPPENED TO MY *HAND*."

"I'M NOT AFRAID, CYRUS," SAYS THE KID.

"*WHAT?*" SAYS CYRUS, TAKEN BACK.

"I MEAN, YOU CAN *TELL ME*," SAYS THE KID. "I'M NOT *AFRAID*."

"HMMM, *OKAY*... LET'S SEE HOW I CAN *TELL* THIS STORY." CYRUS REACHES INTO HIS POCKET. "YOU LIKE *BASEBALL?* YOU EVER HEARD OF *HONUS WAGNER?*"

1989

"WAGNER PITTSBURG!" BILLY SAYS AS HE PICKS THE CARD FROM THE CIGAR BOX." *MAYBE* THIS IS *HIS* STUFF. NO, *WAIT.* IT SAYS *PIEDMONT: THE CIGARETTE OF QUALITY* AND *BASEBALL* SERIES ON THE BACK. I'VE NEVER HEARD OF HIM. *YOU GUYS?"*

"WAGNER PITTSBURG? NOPE." SAYS PETE.

"DUDE, YOU *KNOW* I DON'T KNOW *SHIT* ABOUT SPORTS." SAYS MIKE.

1938

"HONUS WAGNER. *'THE FLYING DUTCHMAN.'* HE WAS THE SHORTSTOP FOR THE *PITTSBURG PIRATES."* CYRUS HANDS THE KID THE CARD. "HE'S WHO *I* WANTED TO BE. I EVEN GOT TO *SEE* HIM PLAY AGAINST *TY COBB* AND THE *TIGERS* IN THE *'09 WORLD SERIES.* MY DAD TOOK ME AND MY SISTER TO GAME SEVEN. *THAT'S* WHEN I DECIDED THAT I WAS GONNA BE A *BALL PLAYER."*

"I COULD SEE HOW *HAPPY* BASEBALL MADE MY DAD. NOT MUCH MADE HIM HAPPY AFTER MY *MA...* " CYRUS GETS CHOKED UP. "WELL, *ANYWAY,* THERE WAS JUST THE *THREE* OF US. MY SISTER DOROTHY LOVED *DANCING,* MY DAD LOVED *BASEBALL,* AND I LOVED MY *DAD.* I *REALIZED* AFTER *THAT* GAME, I COULD MAKE MY DAD HAPPY BY BECOMING THE *BEST* AT BASEBALL. I *DID* JUST THAT. I EVEN MADE IT TO THE *MINORS* BY AGE *NINETEEN.* MY DAD AND SISTER WENT TO *EVERY GAME."*

"I PITCHED FOR THE *PITTSFIELD HILLIES.* WE DID *OKAY.* THERE WAS THIS ONE GAME WHEN TALENT SCOUTS FOR THE *MAJORS* CAME TO SEE ME PLAY. I WAS SO *EXCITED."* CYRUS CONTINUES. *"BUT* THEY WEREN'T THE *ONLY ONES* TO COME SEE ME THAT DAY. RIGHT BEFORE THE GAME, I WAS VISITED BY THE *SCHECKLE BROTHERS.* THE THREE OF THEM OFFERED TO PAY ME TO *LOSE* THE GAME *ON PURPOSE.* IT TURNED OUT THEY WERE RUNNING A SMALL-TIME *GAMBLING RING* AND THIS GAME HAD THE NUMBERS WORKING IN FAVOR OF THE *WORCESTER BOOSTERS,* THE OPPOSING TEAM. IF I THREW THE GAME, THE SCHECKLE BROTHERS WOULD MAKE *A LOT* OF MONEY."

" BUT, I *DIDN'T* THROW THE GAME. *INSTEAD,* I PITCHED THE *BEST* GAME OF MY *LIFE."* CYRUS GOES ON. *"I* THOUGHT OF MY *DAD* AND HOW *DISAPPOINTED* HE WOULD BE IF I THREW THE GAME. I THOUGHT OF THE *TALENT SCOUTS* AND HOW I WOULD BE BLOWING MY FUTURE *CAREER* IN THE MAJORS. I THOUGHT IT WAS THE *RIGHT THING TO DO.* BUT, AT THE END OF THE DAY, AFTER IT *ALL* WENT DOWN, IT WAS *REALLY* ABOUT *PRIDE.* I WANTED TO WIN FOR *ME.* I WASN'T GONNA BE *SWAYED* BY SOME SMALL-TIME *THUGS."*

"BUT WHAT DOES THAT HAVE TO DO WITH YOUR *HAND?"* THE KID ASKS.

"WELL, *SIMPLY* PUT..." CYRUS EXPLAINS." ...WHEN PEOPLE LOSE MONEY, THEY GET *UPSET.* WHEN *BAD* PEOPLE LOSE MONEY, THEY GET *REVENGE.* THE WAY THEY SEE IT: *SOMEONE'S GOTTA PAY.* I NOT ONLY LOST THOSE SCHECKLE BROTHERS *A LOT* OF MONEY, BUT I ALSO COST THEM THE *DEALS* RIDING ON THAT MONEY *BEING* THERE. I *INADVERTENTLY* RUINED THEIR REPUTATIONS, A *BIG* NO-NO."

"AFTER THE GAME SOME OF THE TALENT SCOUTS CAME TO SEE ME. THEY LIKED WHAT THEY SAW. I COULD SEE THE *PRIDE* IN MY DAD'S EYES. I WAS ON *CLOUD NINE."* CYRUS CONTINUES. *"LATER,* AS MY DAD, SISTER AND I WERE HEADING TO OUR CAR, THAT'S WHEN *IT* HAPPENED. THE SCHECKLE BROTHERS WANTED THEIR REVENGE RIGHT *THEN AND THERE.* THINKING ABOUT IT *NOW,* IT ALL HAPPENED SO *FAST.* WHEN IT WAS ALL OVER, MY PITCHING HAND WAS *GONE,* MY FATHER WAS BEATEN TO A *PULP,* AND MY SISTER AND I WERE SENT OFF TO SEE THE *OTHER* SCHECKLE BROTHER."

"OTHER SCHECKLE BROTHER?" THE KID ASKS.

"YEAH, KID. *SLIM."* CYRUS SAYS COLDLY.

1989

"HOLY SHIT, GUYS! IT'S A *GOLD NUGGET RING!"* SAYS BILLY EXCITEDLY.

*"THIS IS LIKE SOME **GODFATHER** TYPE OF RING."* BILLY PUTS IT ON HIS FINGER. *"**DAMN,** IT MAKES ME FEEL ALL **POWERFUL** LIKE **THANOS** OR **GREEN LANTERN!"***

*"**DUDE,** WHO **KNOWS** WHAT THAT THING HAS BEEN THROUGH."* SAYS PETE.

*"IT COULD **TOTALLY** HAVE COME FROM THE **GOLD RUSH!"*** SAYS MIKE.

*"OR BELONGED TO SOME **WIZARD!"*** BILLY JOKES.

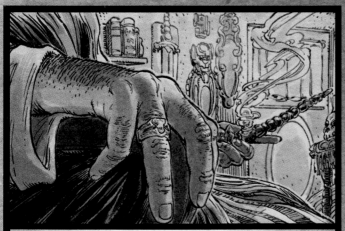

1940
SUMMER

HAZE FILLS THE AIR AS MOSES THE MYSTIC SITS IN AN OPIUM-INDUCED TRANCE. HIS TRANCE IS INTERRUPTED BY PANICKED KNOCKS AT HIS TRAILER DOOR.

KNOCK! KNOCK! KNOCK!

"MOSES!" CYRUS SHOUTS. *"OPEN* THE *DOOR!"*

*"IT'S GETTING **WORSE!"*** EARL ADDS, JUST AS RUSHED.

*"COUGH! COUGH!... JUST... HOLD **ON!"*** MOSES STUMBLES TO THE DOOR AND OPENS IT.

*"**MOSES,** YOUR TONIC **ISN'T** WORKING! THE KID LOOKS **WORSE!"*** SAYS EARL.

*"LEMME... **LEMME...** SEE... **LEMME SEE."*** MOSES FUMBLES HIS WORDS.

*"**CRAP.** MOSES... ARE YOU **DRUNK?!"*** CYRUS SAYS INCREDULOUSLY. *"WE **NEED** YOU!!"*

"OKAY, OKAY..." MOSES CAREFULLY UNWRAPS THE KID'S BANDAGES FROM HIS FACE. "THIS ISN'T AS *BAD* AS IT *LOOKS*..."

"WHAT MAKES YOU SO *SURE?*" CYRUS ASKS.

"*WELL*, BECAUSE IT'S A KIND OF *FUNGUS.*" MOSES REPLIES. "NOT QUITE WHAT I WAS *AIMING* TO DO, *BUT*--"

"--WITH THE *RIGHT* FORMULAIC *ADJUSTMENTS*..." MOSES CONTINUES. "...IT COULD CLEAR UP WITHIN A FEW *WEEKS* TO A COUPLE OF *MONTHS.* THE *MAIN* PROBLEM IS HOW TO BREAK THE NEWS TO *SLIM.*"

"MOSES, YOU NEED TO *SLOW DOWN* ON YOUR '*MIDNIGHT OIL*'." CYRUS SCOLDS. "SLIM HAS BEEN OUT OF TOWN FOR *TWO WEEKS* NOW."

"OUT OF *TOWN?*" MOSES ASKS, CONFUSED. "FOR HOW *LONG?*"

"*INDEFINITELY.*" EARL REPLIES. "AND UNTIL THEN, *I'M* IN CHARGE."

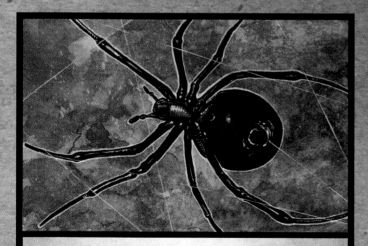

TWO WEEKS EARLIER IN A NEW JERSEY WAREHOUSE.

"WELL, *LOOK* WHO IT IS: *LEON SCHECKLE* IN THE *FLESH.*" A DEEP VOICE ANNOUNCES. "WE *FINALLY* GET TO SEE THE *MAN* BEHIND THE *STORIES!*"

"*HEH*, GOOD TO MEET *YOU* TOO..." SAYS SLIM. "WHERE IS *EDDIE?* HE WAS SUPPOSED TO BE HERE *TOO.*"

"I'M *SURE* WE'LL BE SEEING HIM *SHORTLY.*" SAYS THE DEEP VOICE. "DO YOU HAVE WHAT YOU *OWE* TO *MRS. VALENTINA?*"

"*HEH, THE ROYALTIES.* YES. *OF COURSE*, DEN." SAYS SLIM. "EVERY *NICKEL. SLINK*, WILL YOU BRING OUT THE *CASE?*"

"I'M *SURE* THERE'S *NO NEED* TO COUNT IT," SAYS THE DEEP-VOICED MAN.

MRS. VALENTINA WATCHES FROM THE BACK OF HER *'38 CHEVY.* SLINK MEETS
EYES WITH HER, THEY SHARE A MOMENT AND SHE GIVES A NOD.
SLINK'S HAND SLIDES INTO SLIM'S COAT POCKET.

IT HAPPENS SO FAST.

UNEXPECTED.

EVEN SLIM DOESN'T SEE IT COMING.

AND JUST LIKE THAT, IT IS DONE.

INTO THE *DARKNESS* WE GO.

MRS. VALENTINA GAVE SLIM THE SAME CONSIDERATION THAT SLIM GAVE OTHERS. LIVE BY THE SWORD, DIE BY THE SWORD.

TWO WEEKS LATER AT THE CIRCUS.

"BOY OF WOOD. HEH. YOU AND YOUR *MOVIES,"* CYRUS TEASES EARL. *"*I THINK *THIS* WILL BRING IN A CROWD *MUCH* BETTER. IT'S OKAY KID, YOU CAN OPEN YOUR *EYES* NOW."

" I PRESENT TO YOU *'THE LIZARD-FACED BOY'*! OR *'THE LITTLE DRAGON'*! WHICHEVER YOU PREFER," CYRUS EXCLAIMS. "A LITTLE MORE OF THAT CLOWN MAKEUP ON YOUR *HANDS* AND THE ILLUSION *WORKS!"*

" WHAT DO YOU THINK, *KID?"* ASKS EARL. " IT'S UP TO *YOU*. YOU DON'T *HAVE TO* DO IT."

" I... I... I LOOK SO *COOL!"* SAYS THE KID. " I LIKE *'THE LITTLE DRAGON'*. I'M *THE LITTLE DRAGON!"*

SHOW AFTER SHOW, *"THE LITTLE DRAGON"* IS A SMASH SUCCESS. EVERY DAY SEEMS BETTER THAN THE LAST. NOBODY REALLY WANTS SLIM TO COME BACK. EARL SEEMS TO BE DOING A GREAT JOB BY ALL ACCOUNTS.

OVER THE COURSE OF A MONTH, THE CIRCUS MAKES ITS WAY TOWARDS NEW JERSEY.

"MAMA, DO YOU *MISS* SLIM?" ASKS THE KID.

"NO, MON *CHER*. I DO *NOT."* MILLIE SAYS WITH A SERIOUS TONE.

"WHEN IS HE COMING *BACK?"* THE KID ASKS.

"WHY DO YOU ASK, MY *LOVE?"* MILLIE REPLIES.

"WELL, I WAS THINKING HOW *EVERYBODY* CALLS ME *'KID'*...AND HOW *SLIM* ALWAYS CALLS ME *'EM'* OR *'ET'*... " THE KID PAUSES. "I... MISS *THAT."*

"YOU DO?" MILLIE ASKS. *"WHY?"*

"WELL, BECAUSE IT'S THE CLOSEST THING I'VE GOT TO A NAME. IS IT *SHORT* FOR SOMETHING?" THE KID ASKS. "BECAUSE, I LIKE THE NAME *'EMMETT.'* BUT, IS IT STRANGE FOR PEOPLE TO *MAKE UP* A NAME FOR THEMSELVES?"

"*NO*, MY SWEET, IT ISN'T *AT ALL*," MILLIE SAYS.

"*THEN* I WANT TO BE CALLED *EMMETT* FROM NOW ON, *OKAY?*" SAYS THE KID.

"OKAY, *EMMETT.*" MILLIE SMILES.

THE CARAVAN STARTS TO SLOW DOWN.

"MAMA, *WHY* ARE WE *STOPPING?*" ASKS EMMETT. "*EARL* SAID THIS WAS AN *OVER-NIGHTER.*"

"I *DON'T KNOW*, MY SWEET. *MAYBE* SOMEONE NEEDS *GAS* OR HAS A *FLAT.*" MILLIE REPLIES. "*I'M SURE* IT'S *NOTHING* TO WORRY ABOUT."

THE CARAVAN CONVOY STOPS SO EARL CAN MAKE A PHONE CALL.

"*WHAT?* THAT MAKES *NO SENSE.* HE SAID *JERSEY*," EARL SAYS, FRUSTRATED. "*COLUMBUS?* PUT HIM ON THE PHONE. *WHATDAYA MEAN HE CAN'T TALK?!* THIS IS *BULLSHIT!!* FINE, YES, FINE. *I SAID FINE.* OKAY, SEE YOU THERE THEN."

FOR WHAT SEEMS LIKE MINUTES, ALL THAT CAN BE HEARD IS THE WHITE NOISE OF THE CARS SPEEDING DOWN ROUTE 130. EARL PACES BACK AND FORTH LIKE AN ANGRY LION. THE PRESSURE MOUNTS WITH EACH LAP.

"SON OF A *BITCH!!*" EARL YELLS.

A FEW OF THE CIRCUS TROUPE MEMBERS COME OUT OF THEIR CARAVANS TO SEE WHAT'S GOING ON.

"IT'S *ALL RIGHT* GUYS. *I'M* ALL RIGHT," EARL CALMS THE GROUP. "YOU CAN ALL GO BACK INTO YOUR *CAMPERS*. IF YOU NEED TO DO ANYTHING ELSE WHILE WE'RE HERE, WE ROLL OUT IN *15 MINUTES*."

"WHAT'S GOING ON, *EARL?*" CYRUS ASKS.

"GODDAMN *SLIM*. HE'S OUT OF HIS *MIND*," EARL REPLIES.

"YOU *TALKED* WITH SLIM?" CYRUS ASKS.

"NOT *EXACTLY*. IT WAS SOMEONE FROM '*THE ORGANIZATION*'--" EARL EXPLAINS.

"--THEY SAID TO STOP HEADING TOWARD *TRENTON* AND TO HEAD TO *COLUMBUS* VIA *ROUTE 23*. IT'S *INSANE*. THAT *WHOLE ROUTE* IS *SOGNO* TERRITORY," SAYS EARL.

"YEAH, WE HAVEN'T BEEN ON ROUTE 23 IN ALMOST *8 YEARS* FOR THAT *VERY* REASON. DID THEY SAY *WHY?*" ASKS CYRUS.

"*NOPE*. SLIM WILL MEET US THERE IN COLUMBUS," EARL SAYS BLUNTLY. "I *DUNNO*. MAYBE IT'S A *TRUCE* WITH THE *SOGNO BROTHERS*. WE'LL SOON FIND OUT. LET'S ROLL OUT."

1989

"*LA TOUR EIFFEL!* SWEET *SPOON!*" SAYS BILLY AS HE PULLS THE SILVER SPOON FROM THE CIGAR BOX. "LOOKS *A LOT* LIKE A SET MY GRANDMA THOMPSON HAS. I *REMEMBER* SEEING THEM WHEN WE MOVED INTO HER AND GRANDPA'S HOUSE. *WOW*, MEMORIES."

"I WONDER WHAT'S SO *SPECIAL* ABOUT THIS SPOON, THAT IT'S IN THIS *BOX* WITH THE REST OF THIS *STUFF*," SAYS BILLY.

"PROBABLY BECAUSE IT'S *SILVER*, DUDE," PETE ANSWERS.

"*MAYBE* IT MEANS SOMETHING TO THE PERSON WHO IT *BELONGED TO*..." SAYS BILLY.

"I'M *TELLING* YOU, MAN... THAT'S A BOX FILLED WITH *STORIES*," SAYS PETE.

1940

THE CIRCUS CARAVAN MAKES ITS WAY WEST TOWARD COLUMBUS.

"MAMA, WHAT ARE THESE THINGS IN YOUR SHOEBOX?" ASKS EMMETT.

"'LA TOUR EIFFEL.' THE EIFFEL TOWER..." MILLIE REPLIES.

"WHY DO YOU HAVE SO MANY?" EMMETT ASKS.

"THEY REMIND ME OF THE PAST..." MILLIE REPLIES. "...OF MY DREAMS."

"YOUR DREAMS?" EMMETT ASKS CURIOUSLY.

"OUI, MON CHER," MILLIE GETS SERIOUS. "WHEN I WAS A LITTLE GIRL, GROWING UP IN THE CITY OF LIGHTS."

"THE CITY OF LIGHTS?" EMMETT ASKS.

"OUI, PARIS. THE CAPITAL OF ART AND CULTURE. ALL I EVER WANTED TO BE A DANCER. I WAS YOUNG, THIN, AND BEAUTIFUL. AS YOU CAN SEE FROM THIS PHOTOGRAPH, I HAD STYLE TOO. ONE DAY, I MET A MAN WHO MADE ME FORGET ALL OF MY DREAMS, AND I FOLLOWED HIM HERE TO AMERICA. SOMETHING BAD HAPPENED TO HIM AND I WAS STRANDED WITH ONLY MY DANCING TO MAKE DO. THAT'S WHEN I FOUND THE CIRCUS."

THE WOMAN IN THIS PICTURE ISN'T MILLIE DOUBOIR. IT'S COCO CHANEL. THE PICTURE WAS TORN FROM AN OLD FASHION MAGAZINE AND PUT IN THE EIFFEL TOWER FRAME BY MILLIE. MILLIE ISN'T EVEN HER REAL NAME, AND SHE'S NOT FROM FRANCE, OR EVEN FRENCH FOR THAT MATTER. HER REAL NAME IS DOROTHY PARKER. SHE'S THE LITTLE SISTER OF CYRUS PARKER, THE ONE-HANDED LION TAMER. THERE IS TRUTH IN SOME OF WHAT SHE SAYS. SHE WAS A PROMISING DANCER. THERE WAS A MAN THAT CAME INTO HER LIFE AND MADE HER FORGET ABOUT HER DREAMS. IT JUST ISN'T THE WAY SHE EXPLAINS IT. NOT EVEN CLOSE.

IN 1921 WHEN SLIM "ACQUIRED" DOROTHY AND CYRUS, DOROTHY WAS ONLY 15 YEARS OLD. SLIM PUT HER RIGHT TO WORK AS A *HOOCHIE COOCHIE DANCER*. SHE WAS A NATURAL WITH HER GOOD LOOKS AND DANCING ABILITY. THE ONE PART OF THE SHOW SHE REFUSED WAS TO DO A *"DING"* OR A *"BLOWOFF."* SHE WAS OKAY WITH EXHIBITING HER BODY BECAUSE SHE CONVINCED HERSELF IT WAS *ART.* BEING INTIMATE WITH SIDESHOW PATRONS FOR MONEY, ON THE OTHER HAND, WASN'T SOMETHING SHE WAS WILLING TO DO.

SLIM HAD A PROBLEM WITH THIS.

ADDING TO THE PROBLEM WAS A *FRENCH TRAVELING SALESMAN* WHO TOOK A GENUINE LIKING TOWARDS DOROTHY. HIS SALES ROUTE WAS THE SAME AS SLIM'S CIRCUS, WHICH MADE IT CONVENIENT FOR THE SALESMAN TO SEE DOROTHY. HE BEGAN SHOWING UP NIGHT AFTER NIGHT TO SEE HER. HE TOLD HER THAT HE COULD TAKE HER AWAY, MAKE A GOOD LIFE FOR HER. THEY BEGAN TO MAKE PLANS TO LEAVE THE CIRCUS. THE NIGHT THEY WERE GOING TO MAKE THEIR ESCAPE, THEY WERE STOPPED BY SLIM. HE APPROACHED THE SALESMAN AND TOLD HIM THAT IF HE WANTED A PIECE OF DOROTHY, THAT HE'D HAVE TO PAY. THIS UPSET THE SALESMAN AND IN FRENCH FASHION, HE SLAPPED SLIM ACROSS THE FACE.

THIS SPOON, A FEW PICTURE FRAMES AND AN ASSORTMENT OF OTHER EIFFEL TOWER SOUVENIRS ARE THE ONLY TRACES LEFT OF THE FRENCH SALESMAN. SOME SAY SLIM HAD THE FRENCHMAN DISPOSED OF. SOME SAY THAT SLIM SCARED THE FRENCHMAN OFF. THERE'S ONE THING THAT'S FOR SURE, AND THAT WAS SLIM'S CRUELTY TOWARDS DOROTHY AFTER HER FAILED ESCAPE. INSTEAD OF SCOLDING HER, SLIM GAVE HER ALL OF THE FRENCH SALESMAN'S BELONGINGS AND SAID, "HERE'S YOUR KNIGHT IN SHINING ARMOR." SLIM LAUGHED AND WALKED AWAY. DOROTHY DIDN'T TAKE THE NEWS WELL AND BEGAN TO COMFORT HERSELF BY OVEREATING. SHE DIRECTLY ASSOCIATED THIS SPOON WITH HER LOVE FOR THE SALESMAN AND ATE WITH IT EXCLUSIVELY.

DOROTHY KNEW THAT HER WORTH TO SLIM WAS IN HER DANCING ABILITY AND HER YOUNG, SLENDER FIGURE. SHE KNEW THAT SLIM WOULD MAKE HER STOP DANCING IF SHE GAINED WEIGHT, SO SHE BEGAN TO EAT WHENEVER SHE COULD AND CHANGED HER APPEARANCE DRASTICALLY IN A MATTER OF MONTHS. SLIM IN A RAGE, KICKED HER OFF OF THE HOOCHIE COOCHIE DETAIL. SHE GOT WHAT SHE WANTED. IT WAS SHORT-LIVED. SLIM RETURNED TO HER TENT WITH A BUCKET OF SLOP AND SAID, "YOU AIN'T GONNA EARN FOR ME AS A DANCER?! WELL, DEN, YOU GONNA EAT SLOP AND KEEP GAINING THAT WEIGHT SO I CAN EARN FROM YOUR FAT ASS IN ANOTHER WAY!" AND SO BEGAN DOROTHY'S LIFE AS THE FAT LADY. NIGHT AFTER NIGHT, SLIM FORCE-FED HER. DOROTHY'S MIND COULDN'T TAKE IT, SO SHE BECAME MILLIE DOUBOIR, THE PARISIAN FAT LADY IN NOT JUST BODY, BUT MIND AS WELL.

MILLIE CARRIES ON WITH HER STORY AS THE CIRCUS CONVOY MAKES ITS WAY TOWARD COLUMBUS.

MEANWHILE, CYRUS AND EARL HAVE A DISCUSSION OF THEIR OWN.

"SO WHAT DO YOU THINK SLIM'S *BIG NEWS* IS?" EARL ASKS.

"YOU KNOW, THE ONE THING ABOUT SLIM; HE'S *ALWAYS* GOT A TRICK UP HIS SLEEVE," CYRUS REPLIES.

"WHICH IS *WHY* I HAVE A BAD FEELING ABOUT THIS," SAYS EARL. "WE'LL NEED TO STAY *ALERT*. THIS *ALL* SEEMS OUT OF CHARACTER. EVEN FOR SLIM."

"*AGREED*," SAYS CYRUS.

"*ALL RIGHT*, THIS IS THE RIGHT *GATE*," SAYS EARL. "WHO THE *HELL* IS THIS *GUY?*"

THE MAN AT THE GATE DOESN'T SAY A WORD. HE HANDS EARL A NOTE WITH DETAILED INSTRUCTIONS OF WHAT TO DO AND WHERE TO GO: LEAVE THE CONVOY THERE AT THE GATE AND HEAD TO THE OLD CANNERY, JUST TWO-MILES DOWN THE ACCESS ROAD ON THE LEFT. PULL THE TRUCK INTO WAREHOUSE NUMBER TWENTY-ONE AND WAIT.

EARL SETTLES THE CONVOY AT THE GATE THEN HE AND CYRUS MAKE THEIR WAY TO THE CANNERY.

"MAMA, HOW *LONG* ARE WE GONNA STAY HERE?" EMMETT ASKS.

"I'M NOT SURE, MY SWEET," MILLIE REPLIES. "WE CAN ASK CYRUS IN THE *MORNING*. NOW GET TO *SLEEP*."

KNOCK! **KNOCK!** KNOCK! MILLIE'S CARAVAN DOOR SHAKES.

"GO CHECK TO SEE WHO THAT *IS*, MON CHER." SAYS MILLIE.

"WHO IS IT, MY SWEET?" MILLIE ASKS.

"THERE'S *NOBODY* HERE, MAMA. JUST SOME *BOX* WITH A *NOTE* ON IT," EMMETT REPLIES.

"WHAT DOES IT *SAY?"* MILLIE ASKS.

"IT SAYS *'FOR THE KID'* AND THAT'S *ALL,"* SAYS EMMETT.

"I WONDER *WHO* LEFT IT?" *SAYS MILLIE.* "OPEN IT AND LET'S *SEE."*

THE MAN FROM THE GATE WATCHES FROM THE SHADOWS BEFORE HE RIDES OFF INTO THE DARKNESS.

MEANWHILE, DOWN THE ROAD AT WAREHOUSE TWENTY-ONE.

"I'M *TIRED* OF WAITING," SAYS CYRUS.

" WELL, THE NOTE *SAID* TO PULL THE TRUCK *IN,"* SAYS EARL. *"OPEN* THE DOOR UP, AND LET'S *GO IN."*

CYRUS GETS OUT AND OPENS THE WAREHOUSE DOOR.

"HELLO?" CYRUS CALLS INSIDE." THERE *ISN'T* ANYBODY *HERE. WAIT...* THERE'S *ANOTHER* NOTE. WHAT THE HELL IS GOING ON HERE?"

THE MEN READ THE NOTE.

DEAR MR. HASTINGS,
APOLOGIES FOR THE ESPIONAGE. YOU SEE, IT WAS ALL VERY NECESSARY. MY NAME IS GIANNA VALENTINA. I RECENTLY ACQUIRED THE SOGNO BROS CIRCUS, AND EVEN MORE RECENTLY, TOOK OVER LEON SCHECKLE'S SHARE OF SLIM'S BIG SHOW. ALL I REALLY WANTED WAS THE DOG AND CAT ACT. SEEING AS THE DOG IS NOW A DRAGON, THAT WON'T DO. AS OF NOW, THE SOGNO BROS GET SLIM'S OLD ROUTE AND YOU GET ROUTE 23. YOU NOW OWE ME $100,000. I'M GIVING YOU EXACTLY TEN YEARS TO PAY IT BACK. WITH INTEREST.
-V

P.S. INSIDE THE CRATE IS WHAT'S LEFT OF LEON SCHECKLE. YOUR TIGER IS GOING TO EAT WELL FOR A WHILE. CONSIDER THIS A GIFT.

"WHY AREN'T YOU *SAYING* ANYTHING?" CYRUS ASKS. "C'MON, *ADMIT IT.* THIS IS A REAL *STRETCH*, EVEN FOR SLIM. WOULDN'T YOU SAY?"

"*NO.* NO, IF THIS IS *REAL*, WHICH I'M PRETTY SURE *IT IS*, WE ARE *FUCKED.* NOT JUST *KIND OF*," EARL SAYS. "WE'RE GOING TO *WANT* TO PAY THAT $100,000. JUST LIKE SHE SAYS. THAT IS, *UNLESS* WE WANT TO END UP IN *CANS* TOO."

"WHO *IS* SHE?" ASKS CYRUS.

EARL TAKES A MOMENT. *"THE DEVIL."*

THE MEN PACK THE CRATE INTO THE BACK OF THE TRUCK AND HEAD BACK TO THE CAMP. THE TWO-MILE DRIVE FEELS LIKE HOURS. NEITHER MAN SAYS A WORD ON THE DRIVE.

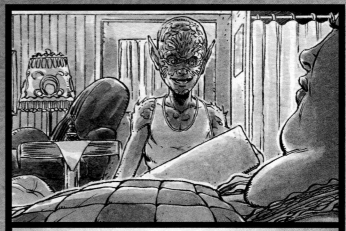

MEANWHILE, BACK AT THE CAMP...

"IT FEELS LIKE THERE'S SOMETHING *ROLLING AROUND* IN THERE," SAYS EMMETT. "IT'S *NOT* THAT *HEAVY.*"

"WELL *HURRY UP* AND *OPEN IT,* MON CHER!" SAYS MILLIE.

KNOCK! **KNOCK!**

"ANOTHER VISITOR? OR MAYBE YOUR *'FRIEND'* CAME BACK?" SAYS MILLIE.

"CYRUS! YOU'RE BACK!" EMMETT SAYS EXCITEDLY.

"HEY, KID," SAYS CYRUS. "MILLIE, *LOOK,* WE GOTTA *TALK.* THIS IS *SERIOUS."*

"COME IN. *COME IN,"* SAYS MILLIE. "YOU LOOK LIKE YOU'VE SEEN A *GHOST!"*

CYRUS TELLS HIS SISTER WHAT HE AND EARL SAW AT THE CANNERY WAREHOUSE.

"DON'T YOU *SEE?* WE'RE *FREE!* WE CAN *GO* NOW," SAYS CYRUS.

"CYRUS, WE'VE BEEN HERE FOR ALMOST *TWENTY YEARS.* WHAT WOULD WE *DO?"* MILLIE ASKS. "YOU CAN'T *PITCH.* I CAN'T *DANCE. THIS LIFE* IS ALL WE KNOW. FROM WHAT YOU'RE SAYING ABOUT THIS *VALENTINA,* I DON'T THINK SHE WILL *LET US* LEAVE. BESIDES, HOW DO YOU *KNOW* THAT SLIM IS *REALLY* GONE?"

"HEY, LOOK!" EMMETT SAYS WITH JOY.

ANY DOUBT ABOUT SLIM'S DEATH IS EXTINGUISHED THAT VERY MOMENT.

1989

"YEAH! *NOW* WE'RE TALKING," BILLY SAYS EXCITEDLY. "SOME SORT OF *MINI-COMIC...*"

"LEMME SEE!" SAYS MIKE.

"*CHECK IT OUT!* IT LOOKS LIKE SOME JAPANESE *CALVIN AND HOBBES* COMIC!" SAYS BILLY.

"DUDE, I DIDN'T EVEN *KNOW* THEY HAD THAT IN JAPAN," SAYS MIKE.

"*GUYS,* IT'S PROBABLY SOME SORT OF *KNOCK-OFF,*" SAYS PETE.

"*MAN,* I WISH I KNEW WHAT IT *SAID,*" SAYS BILLY.

"WELL, IF THE *STORYTELLING'S* ANY GOOD, YOU *SHOULD* BE ABLE TO TELL WHAT'S GOING ON *WITHOUT* THE WORDS," SAYS MIKE.

1949

EMMETT IS IN THE MIDDLE OF AN AGE OLD RITE OF PASSAGE FOR A YOUNG ROUSTABOUT: *DOING ROCKS.* DOING ROCKS INVOLVES THE SEARCH AND COLLECTION OF LARGE ROCKS, WHICH ARE USED TO BUILD SMALL PILES. SOMETIMES DOING ROCKS FACILITATES THE CLEARING OF AN AREA SO THAT A TENT OR RIDE CAN BE PUT THERE. OTHER TIMES, DOING ROCKS IS ASSIGNED AS BUSY WORK FOR ROUSTABOUTS WITH NOTHING BETTER TO DO. TODAY IT'S BUSY WORK.

EMMETT PUTS THE LAST ROCK ON THE PILE WHEN HE GETS THE MOST UNEXPECTED VISITOR.

"EXCUSE ME, *YOUNG MAN,*" A VOICE SAYS IN AN ACCENT. "PERHAPS YOU CAN TELL ME?"

"UM, YES, SIR. I CAN DO MY *BEST* TO *TRY,*" EMMETT REPLIES. "WHAT MAY I HELP YOU WITH?"

"COULD YOU PLEASE LEAD ME TO A *MR. SLIM?*" THE VOICE REPLIES.

"*SLIM?*" THE NAME EMMETT HASN'T SAID OR HEARD IN YEARS, "DO YOU MEAN *EARL?*"

"IS HE *IN CHARGE* OF THIS CIRCUS?" THE MAN WITH THE ACCENT ASKS.

"YES," EMMETT REPLIES.

"THEN *THAT'S* WHO I NEED TO SEE," SAYS THE MAN. "I HAVE *NEWS.*"

"I GOTTA BE *HONEST,* CYRUS, I'M *SCARED,*" EARL SAYS WITH CONCERN. "IN *NINE YEARS,* WE'VE NEVER MISSED A PAYMENT. WITHOUT A *FEATURE* WE'RE ONLY MAKING *HALF* OF WHAT WE *WERE* MAKING."

"WELL, THERE ARE ONLY REALLY *TWO* OPTIONS..." SAYS CYRUS. "...ASK FOR AN *EXTENSION* OR PRAY FOR A *MIRACLE.*"

"*PFT.* IT'LL BE A *MIRACLE* TO SEE *VALENTINA* GIVE *ANYONE* AN EXTENSION," SAYS EARL.

"HEY, *EARL,* THERE'S SOMEONE HERE TO SEE YOU," SAYS EMMETT.

"GUYS, THIS IS *HIROFUMI TEKKA.* HE SAYS HE CAME HERE ALL OF THE WAY FROM *JAPAN* TO SEE *SLIM,*" EMMETT SAYS. "SAYS HE *HAS SOMETHING* FOR HIM."

"HELLO, MR. TEKKA. I'M *REAL SORRY* YOU CAME *ALL OF THIS WAY.* SLIM ISN'T HERE AND *WON'T BE* FOR THE FORESEEABLE FUTURE," SAYS EARL. "ANYTHING *WE* CAN HELP YOU WITH?"

"ARE YOU RESPONSIBLE FOR THE *DOG AND CAT SHOW?*" HIROFUMI ASKS. "THE ONE WITH THE *DOG BOY AND TIGER?*"

"*YES,* THAT'S *US.* THAT WAS OUR *IDEA* AND OUR *SHOW.* BUT WE HAVEN'T DONE IT IN A *LONG TIME,*" SAYS EARL.

"IT *HAS* BEEN A LONG TIME SINCE MY *LAST* VISIT," SAYS HIROFUMI. "IT IS MY *HONOR* TO GIVE YOU *THIS* AND A *GREATER HONOR* TO FINALLY MEET *YOU.*"

"WHAT IS IT?" CYRUS ASKS.

"IT IS THE *PAYMENT* OWED FOR THE USE OF *YOUR* IDEA," HIROFUMI REPLIES.

"THE *USE* OF OUR IDEA?" EARL ASKS. "HOW DO YOU *MEAN?*"

"*TEN* YEARS AGO, I SAW *THE DOG AND CAT SHOW.* IT REMINDED ME OF A *CARTOON.* I MAKE *MANGA.* SO I SAY '*AH-HA!*' AND GO AND VISIT MR. SLIM *THE CIRCUS BOSS.*" HIROFUMI EXPLAINS. "I TELL HIM THAT I WANT TO MAKE A *MANGA* OF *THE DOG AND CAT SHOW...*"

"A *MANGA?*" CYRUS ASKS.

"MANGA ARE COMICS CREATED IN *JAPAN.*" HIROFUMI TAKES OUT THE COMIC. "THIS IS *THE DOG AND CAT MANGA.*"

"MR. SLIM SAYS I CAN MAKE *MANGA*, BUT THAT I MUST PAY A *PERCENTAGE*. I *AGREE*," HIROFUMI SAYS WITH CONFIDENCE. "BUT, THEN THE *WAR* CAME AND I *COULD NOT* RETURN. UNTIL *NOW*."

"*WHY* DIDN'T YOU JUST *STAY* IN *JAPAN*?" CYRUS ASKS.

"BECAUSE I AM AN *HONORABLE MAN*," HIROFUMI SAYS. "AND HE SAID THAT HE WOULD *BREAK MY FINGERS* IF I *DID NOT* HONOR THE DEAL. I *BELIEVED HIM*. THE MANGA IS A *SUCCESS*. *DOG AND CAT MANGA* EVEN HAS *ENDORSEMENTS*."

"THERE ARE *TOYS, GAMES, TREATS* AND *OTHER* ITEMS. IN *FACT*, I BROUGHT ONE HERE AS A *GIFT* FOR THE *DOG BOY*. HE'D BE ABOUT *SIXTEEN*?" HIROFUMI GUESSES. "*IS HE STILL* AROUND?"

"*YES*, IN FACT, YOU'VE *ALREADY* MET HIM," SAYS EARL. "HE'S RIGHT *BEHIND* YOU."

"HEH. HELLO *AGAIN*," EMMETT SAYS SHEEPISHLY. "A *MANGA*, HUH? THAT'S *REALLY* NEAT."

"*WOW!* IT *IS* YOU! I SHOULD HAVE GUESSED BY THE LOOK OF YOUR *EARS*. YOUR *HAIR* IS *GONE* TOO!" SAYS HIROFUMI.

"IT KINDA FELL OUT A FEW YEARS BACK, MR. TEKKA," SAYS EMMETT.

"*PLEASE*, CALL ME *HIRO*. THIS IS WHAT MY *FRIENDS* CALL ME," HIRO SAYS IN EARNEST. "ALL OF THE YEARS OF DRAWING YOU, I FEEL LIKE I *KNOW* YOU!"

"*YEAH?*" ASKS EMMETT.

"*YES*. MR. SLIM TELL ME *EVERYTHING*. HOW HE *BOUGHT* YOU WHEN YOU WERE A *BABY*, HOW YOU WERE A *BIG* SUCCESS AS *THE WOLF BOY*, AND THEN *SUPER-STARDOM* AS *THE DOG BOY* IN *THE DOG AND CAT SHOW*," HIRO ALMOST CAN'T CONTAIN HIMSELF. "*OH, YES*, AND HERE IS A *GIFT* FOR YOU!"

"*BOUGHT* ME?" THE WORDS ECHO THROUGH EMMETT'S MIND.

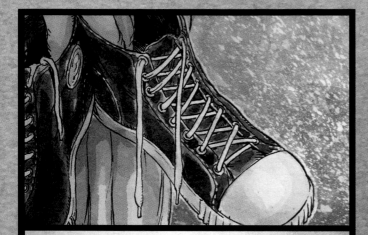

NOT MUCH LATER, BACK IN MILLIE AND EMMETT'S TRAILER.

"I CAN SEE *WHY* THE SHOE COMPANY WOULD *WANT* THE ENDORSEMENT. THE SHOES ARE CALLED *'TIGERS.'* THEY ARE *VERY* NICE, EMMETT," SAYS MILLIE. "*EMMETT?* ARE YOU *OKAY,* SWEETHEART?"

"I'M NOT YOUR SON. I WAS BOUGHT BY SLIM?" EMMETT SAYS, HOLDING BACK HIS EMOTIONS.

"*...OUI.* IT'S TRUE," MILLIE REPLIES, GETTING TO HER FEET.

"YOU *KNEW* THIS WHOLE TIME?" EMMETT SAYS, LETTING HIS EMOTIONS GO. "HOW *MUCH?* HOW MUCH WAS I *BOUGHT* FOR?"

"OH, *MON CHER.* THIS WAS SO *LONG AGO,*" MILLIE TRIES TO EXPLAIN. "WHEN SLIM BOUGHT YOU, I *KNEW* THAT YOU WOULD NEED TO HAVE A *FAMILY.* NOT JUST BE ONE OF HIS *FREAKS.* I BECAME YOUR *FAMILY.*"

"*FAMILY. WHY* WOULD SOMEONE *SELL* THEIR BABY?" EMMETT HOLDS BACK TEARS. "WAS I NOT *GOOD ENOUGH?*"

"*NO, NO, NO,* MON CHER," SAYS MILLIE. "*NEVER* THINK THAT. *EVER.*"

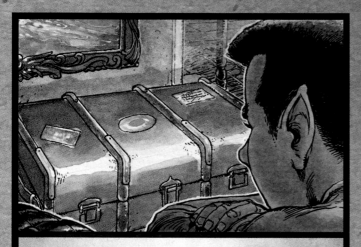

"WHEN YOU CAME TO US, YOU WERE PACKED IN *THAT* TRUNK WITH *EVERYTHING* A BABY COULD NEED. THIS IS *NOT* SOMETHING THAT A *LOVELESS* PERSON DOES," MILLIE CONTINUES. "*NO.* TIMES WERE VERY *HARD* WHEN YOU WERE BORN. WHOEVER YOUR PARENTS *WERE,* SOLD YOU TO SLIM BECAUSE OF HAVING *NO OTHER* CHOICE. I AM *CERTAIN* THIS *MUST* BE WHAT HAPPENED."

EMMETT'S ATTENTION TURNS TO THE TRUNK. HE USED TO SLEEP IN IT. HE KEEPS HIS THINGS IN IT. HE'S RECENTLY STARTED PUTTING STICKERS FROM THE TOWNS HE'S BEEN IN ON IT. BUT THERE'S ONE STICKER THAT'S BEEN THERE SINCE BEFORE HE CAN REMEMBER

THE LUGGAGE TAG. EMMETT USED TO PICK AT IT AND TEAR PIECES OFF OF IT WHEN HE WAS A BABY. HE'S NOW REALIZING THAT IT MAY BE THE ONLY LINK TO LEARNING ABOUT HIS PAST. HE TAKES NOTE OF THE ADDRESS:

1214 WARREN ST.
ASHLAND.

"ASHLAND? BUT, WHICH ONE?" EMMETT THINKS TO HIMSELF. "THERE ARE *TWO* ON ROUTE 23. *KENTUCKY* AND *VIRGINIA.*"

"EARL, WHICH *ASHLAND* IS *CLOSER* TO HERE?" EMMETT ASKS. "*KENTUCKY* OR *VIRGINIA?*"

"*KENTUCKY.* IT'S ABOUT THREE SHOW STOPS FROM HERE," EARL REPLIES.

"HOW LONG IS THAT IN *TIME?*" EMMETT ASKS.

"WELL, KIDDO, *THAT* DEPENDS ENTIRELY ON HOW *FAST* WE EARN MONEY IN EACH TOWN," EARL EXPLAINS. "EVERY TOWN IS *DIFFERENT* AND WITH THAT, YOUR *NUT,* YOUR REQUIRED *BOTTOM LINE* FOR EACH TOWN, IS *DIFFERENT.* THERE ARE DIFFERENT *FEES* AND *TAXES.* IT'S A BUNCH OF COMPLICATED *CRAP, BUT* SUMMING IT UP, THE *FASTER* WE MAKE MONEY, THE FASTER WE CAN *MOVE.*"

"SO *THAT'S* WHY THE SHOW SEEMS TO BE MOVING *SLOWER,*" EMMETT'S WHEELS START TO TURN." IF I WERE TO *FEATURE* AGAIN, WE COULD MAKE *MORE* MONEY!"

"*FEATURE,* KID?" EARL GETS SERIOUS. "NO OFFENSE, BUT THE *REASON* I'VE GOT YOU AS A *ROUSTABOUT* IS SO THAT YOU'RE *CONTRIBUTING* TO THE SHOW IN *SOME* WAY. YOU MAY BE SPECIAL TO *US,* BUT WITHOUT THE *HAIR* OR *SCALES,* YOU'RE JUST *ANOTHER* KID TO THE *REST* OF THE WORLD."

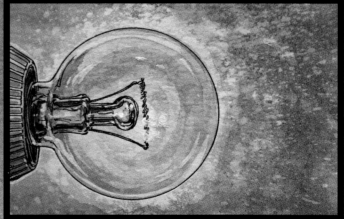

"EARL, IT'S A *SHOW!*" SAYS EMMETT. "I WAS NEVER A *DOG* OR A *DRAGON.* BUT *THAT'S* WHAT PEOPLE PAID TO SEE; *THE SHOW.* THE PRETEND PART."

"*HMM*... KID, YOU KNOW WHAT, YOU'VE GIVEN ME AN *IDEA,*" SAYS EARL. "GO AND GET HIRO. WE'RE GOING INTO TOWN FOR A COUPLE OF HOURS."

AN *IDEA.* THAT'S ALL EMMETT NEEDS.

EARL TAKES EMMETT AND HIRO TO THE ONE PLACE WHERE PROBLEMS SEEM TO MELT AWAY. IT'S EARL'S FAVORITE PLACE: THE MOVIE SHOW. TODAY, THEY'RE IN LUCK. IT'S A *DOUBLE FEATURE.*

POPCORN. IT'S NOT SOMETHING THAT A CIRCUS WORKER USUALLY ENJOYS. MOVIE POPCORN ON THE OTHER HAND, IS SOMETHING ENTIRELY DIFFERENT. BY THE TIME THE FIRST FEATURE, 1943'S *"FRANKENSTEIN MEETS THE WOLF MAN"* IS FINISHED, EARL AND THE GUYS CONSUME MORE THAN THEIR SHARE.

"EARL, WHY ARE YOU WEARING YOUR *EYEPATCH* INSTEAD OF YOUR *GLASS EYE?*" EMMETT ASKS.

"I DUNNO, KID. I GUESS I FEEL LIKE I SEE BETTER *WITH* THE PATCH," EARL REPLIES. *"BESIDES,* THE GLASS EYE IS JUST FOR WHEN WE'RE *WORKING.* RIGHT NOW, WE'RE *NOT* WORKING."

THE SECOND FEATURE, 1943'S *"SON OF DRACULA"* STARS *LON CHANEY, JR.* AS *ALUCARD.* IT'S THE FIRST TIME ON SCREEN WHERE A VAMPIRE IS SHOWN TRANSFORMING INTO A BAT. THE GUYS FIND THIS FASCINATING. IT'S DIFFERENT DETAILS HOWEVER, THAT END UP THE TOPIC OF DISCUSSION AFTER THE FILM.

"I STILL THINK IT WAS AN ODD CHOICE FOR *CHANEY* TO HAVE *DRACULA* WEARING A *MUSTACHE,"* SAYS EARL. "I ALWAYS SAW HIM AS A *SMOOTH FACED* LADY-KILLER."

"I JUST WANT TO KNOW *WHY* THE MOVIE IS CALLED *'SON'* OF DRACULA," SAYS EMMETT. "WE NEVER *ACTUALLY* GET TO SEE HIS SON!"

"YOU *HAVE* TO ADMIT THAT SEEING *BELA LUGOSI* AND *LON CHANEY JR.* DUKE IT OUT WAS *PRETTY COOL,"* SAYS EMMETT. "I STILL PREFER *BORIS KARLOFF* AS *FRANKENSTEIN'S MONSTER.*"

"I *AGREE,* KIDDO," SAYS EARL. "MAYBE *THAT'S* THE KEY: WE CAN *RECAST YOU* AS THE *WOLF* AGAIN. IT'LL TAKE SOME *HEAVY* MAKEUP. BUT, THAT *WON'T* BE GOOD FOR THE *SCHEDULE...*"

"YOU TWO ARE *TRULY* STUCK IN THE JAR." SAYS HIRO.

"THAT SOME *FORTUNE COOKIE* MUMBO JUMBO, *HIRO?"* EARL ASKS.

"*HA,* NO. BUT IT IS *PART* OF A SAYING THAT FITS THIS MOMENT," SAYS HIRO. "' IT IS DIFFICULT TO SEE THE LABEL WHEN YOU ARE INSIDE THE JAR.' YOU TWO ARE *INSIDE* THE JAR. YOU ARE SAYING *EVERYTHING* IT TAKES FOR A NEW *IDEA.* A NEW *SHOW* FOR EMMETT. YOU ARE SAYING IT, BUT YOU ARE NOT *SEEING* IT. I PRESENT TO YOU: *THE VAMPIRE PRINCE!* WITH SOME MAKEUP YOU COULD LIGHTEN YOUR SKIN TO LOOK PALE AND WITH SOME MAGICIAN *TRICKS* YOU COULD TURN INTO A *BAT.* THE WAY MY EYES VIEW IT, YOU HAVE BEEN *THE WOLF* AND *THE MONSTER,* SO *WHY NOT* A *VAMPIRE?*"

EMMETT AND EARL LOOK AT EACH OTHER, AMAZED.

1989

"OH, *WOW.* CHECK *THIS* OUT," SAYS BILLY. "IT'S A POSTER FOR A *MOVIE* OR SOMETHING."

"*'THE VAMPIRE PRINCE.'* YEAH, BUT WHERE ARE THE *CREDITS?*" ASKS MIKE.

"*GUYS.* I TOTALLY FEEL LIKE I'VE SEEN THIS BEFORE," SAYS PETE.

"YEAH, BECAUSE IT LOOKS *A LOT* LIKE BILLY," SAYS MIKE.

"WELL, THERE'S THAT. *WAIT,* YEAH, HE KINDA *DOES.* BUT THAT'S NOT WHAT I *MEAN,*" SAYS PETE. "IT WAS IN *TOWN* AT ONE OF THE *ANTIQUE SHOPS.* I'M NOT *TOTALLY* SURE, BUT I'M PRETTY SURE."

"MAYBE IT WAS A *'THING'* BACK IN THE DAY," BILLY GUESSES.

1950
ASHLAND, VIRGINIA.

"I'M *SURE* MANY OF YOU ARE PLANNING TO GO SEE THIS *'CIRCUS,'*" SAYS THE REVEREND TO HIS FLOCK. "I *URGE* YOU TO *NOT GO!* IT IS *CLEAR* THAT THIS SHOW IS *SATAN'S* HANDIWORK. THEY DON'T EVEN TRY TO *HIDE* IT. *'THE VAMPIRE PRINCE'!* THIS IS A *DEMON!* A *CHILD* OF THE *DEVIL* HIMSELF!"

"I TELL YOU *THIS,*" THE REVEREND GOES ON. "THE *BAT BOY* IS *TROUBLE!*"

"I WANT TO BE IN *TROUBLE,*" WHISPERS A RAVEN-HAIRED GIRL. "HE'S AN ABSOLUTE *DREAMBOAT!*"

THE RAVEN-HAIRED GIRL IS BETSY HARLOW. THE GIRL SHE'S WHISPERING TO IS HER BEST FRIEND, SHELLY MEYERS. THE GUY IN BACK, WHO'S LISTENING INTENTLY TO THE REVEREND IS SHELLY'S TWIN BROTHER TOMMY.

"*BETSY!* SHHH! I MEAN, YEAH, HE *IS* CUTE, BUT HE'S *DANGEROUS!*" SAYS SHELLY.

MEANWHILE, OUTSIDE...

"DID THEY SAY '*GO RIGHT* AT WRIGHT' OR WAS IT 'AT WRIGHT, GO *LEFT*'?" EMMETT SAYS TO HIMSELF AS HE WANDERS THE STREETS OF ASHLAND.

EMMETT SCANS THE STREETS INTENTLY, NOT NOTICING THAT HE'S ABOUT TO RUN INTO SHELLY MEYERS.

"*OOMPH!* OH, MY. I AM *SO* SORRY," SAYS EMMETT, EMBARRASSED.

"*AHGH!* YOU NEARLY *KILLED* US!" SHELLY STIFLES HERSELF.

"OH, I'M SORRY. THAT WAS *IMPOLITE*," SAYS SHELLY. "*HERE*, YOU DROPPED *THIS*."

"*NO*, I'VE GOT IT," SAYS EMMETT, STILL NOT REALLY PAYING ATTENTION.

"I, *UH*... UM," EMMETT SEES SHELLY, AND FOR A MOMENT, TIME IS FROZEN.

"*YES?*" SHELLY HOLDS HER GAZE.

"*YEAH*, SORRY," EMMETT REPLIES. "DO YOU KNOW WHICH WAY IS *WARREN* STREET?"

"YES, IT'S *THAT* WAY," SAYS SHELLY. "IT'S THE FIRST LEFT ON *WRIGHT*."

"*OK.* THANK YOU," EMMETT SMILES. "HAVE A *WONDERFUL* DAY."

"WELL, *SOMEBODY* HAS A CRUSH," BETSY WHISPERS.

"I DO *NOT!*" SHELLY ANSWERS, ALMOST TOO QUICKLY.

"I WASN'T TALKING ABOUT *YOU*," BETSY LAUGHS.

"HE MUST BE VISITING SOMEONE IN TOWN," SAYS SHELLY. "*I'VE* NEVER SEEN HIM BEFORE."

"'*THE VAMPIRE PRINCE.*' WOULD YOU JUST *LOOK* AT HIM?" SAYS BETSY. "WE SHOULD GO TO THE CIRCUS AFTER FRIDAY'S GAME."

"*BETSY!*" SHELLY FEIGNS SHOCK. "THE REVEREND SAID *'NO!'* IT'S *'SATAN'S HANDIWORK.'*"

"*C'MON.* WOULDN'T YOU LIKE TO SEE A *REAL* LIVE VAMPIRE PRINCE?" BETSY ASKS.

"DO YOU THINK HE'S A *REAL* VAMPIRE?" SHELLY ASKS.

"DOES IT *MATTER?*" BETSY REPLIES.

THE GIRLS CONTINUE WALKING AS TOMMY FOLLOWS.

1989

"THERE'S NOT MUCH *ELSE* IN THIS CIGAR BOX EXCEPT THIS *NOTEBOOK*. BUT IT LOOKS LIKE IT'S WRITTEN IN SOME OTHER *LANGUAGE*," SAYS BILLY. "LET'S SEE WHAT'S UNDER THIS *QUILT*."

"*DUDE*, IT LOOKS LIKE SOME KID'S OLD *STUFF*," SAYS MIKE.

"IT'S LIKE A TRUNK FULL OF SOMEONE'S *CHILDHOOD*," SAYS PETE.

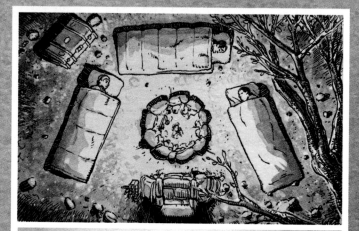

"I WONDER WHY SOMEONE WOULD WANT TO BURY THEIR *STUFF* OUT HERE LIKE THAT," SAYS MIKE.

"*MAYBE*, THEY WANTED TO REMEMBER THE *GOOD TIMES*, LIKE *WE'RE* DOING," SAYS PETE.

"YEAH, LIKE A *TIME CAPSULE*," SAYS BILLY." WE *DEFINITELY* HAVE TO MAKE ONE IN THE *MORNING*. TOO *COOL*. ALL RIGHT, GUYS. NIGHT."

"*NIGHT*, DUDE," PETE AND MIKE SAY IN UNISON.

"*JINX.*"

1950

"*THAT GAVE ME *CHILLS!*" SAYS BETSY. "THE WAY HE WAS *LOOKING* AT US, LIKE HE WANTED TO *BITE* US. THEN TURNING INTO A *BAT!* SO *MYSTERIOUS!*"

"HE *WAS* LOOKING AT US WEIRD. MAYBE HE *DID* WANT TO BITE US!" SAYS SHELLY. "*SPEAKING* OF WHICH, I'M *STARVED*. I'M GONNA FIND SOME FOOD. WANT ANYTHING?"

"NO, I'M OKAY," BETSY REPLIES.

SHELLY MAKES HER WAY DOWN THE MIDWAY. THE SMELL OF FRIED FOOD HAS HER DISTRACTED WHEN SUDDENLY SHE'S STOPPED BY A FAMILIAR FACE.

"*HEY!* HELLO. *AGAIN*," SAYS EMMETT. "DID YOU LIKE THE *SHOW?* I THOUGHT I SAW YOU IN THE CROWD."

SHELLY PAUSES, THEN IT COMES TO HER. "*YOU'RE* THE BOY WHO NEEDED *DIRECTIONS*," SHE SAYS.

"YOU LOOK *DIFFERENT*," EMMETT SAYS. "AH, YOU CUT YOUR *HAIR!*"

"AND, *YOU*, YOU..." SHELLY LOOKS EMMETT OVER. "WAIT A MINUTE. WHAT ARE YOU *WEARING?*"

"OH, *THIS*. I'VE GOT TO KEEP *COVERED* SO I DON'T RUIN THE *ILLUSION*," EMMETT REPLIES.

"*ILLUSION?*" THAT'S WHEN SHE NOTICES. "*YOU'RE THE BAT BOY!*"

"DON'T *WORRY*, I'M NOT GONNA *BITE* YOU... AH?" EMMETT WAITS FOR A REPLY. "WHAT'S YOUR *NAME?*"

SHELLY SNAPS OUT OF HER INITIAL SHOCK. *"SORRY,"* SHE SAYS. *"IT'S SHELLY."*

"HI, SHELLY. I'M EMMETT," EMMETT STRAIGHTENS UP TO SEEM PROPER. *"WHAT ARE YOU UP TO THIS FINE EVENING?"*

"I WAS LOOKING FOR FOOD. I'M STARVED," SHE REPLIES.

"YOU DON'T WANT THE FOOD HERE. THE GREASE WE USE IS PREHISTORIC," SAYS EMMETT. *"I SAW A DINER IN TOWN. LET ME TAKE YOU THERE. MY TREAT."*

"ARE YOU ASKING ME ON A DATE?" ASKS SHELLY.

"I BELIEVE I AM," EMMETT SMILES.

TWO HOURS LATER.

"THANK YOU FOR THE MEAL, EMMETT," SAYS SHELLY. *"I'M GLAD YOU LIKED THE GARLIC FRIES SO MUCH. SORRY ABOUT TEASING YOU. IT'S JUST THAT YOUR SHOW IS REALLY CONVINCING."*

"THANK YOU," EMMETT SMILES. *"IT'S A LOT OF FUN PLAYING A VAMPIRE EACH NIGHT."*

"HEY, DID YOU EVER FIND YOUR FRIEND'S HOUSE?" SHELLY ASKS.

"WHO? FRIEND?...OH! ON WARREN STREET," EMMETT RECALLS. *"YES. I FOUND THE HOUSE, BUT NO ONE WAS HOME. I'M GOING TO TRY AGAIN TOMORROW MORNING."*

AFTER THE ANTI-VAMPIRE CHURCH SERVICE, TOMMY MEYERS SPENT THE WEEK READING UP ON ALL HE COULD FIND ON VAMPIRES. HE LEARNED ABOUT THEIR POWERS, THEIR STRENGTHS AND THEIR WEAKNESSES. IT WASN'T UNTIL AFTER BETSY HARLOW TOLD TOMMY THAT HIS SISTER LEFT THE CIRCUS WITH A 'DARK STRANGER' THAT TOMMY CONSIDERED PUTTING HIS NEWFOUND KNOWLEDGE INTO PRACTICAL APPLICATION.

"WE FOLLOW THEM," SAYS TOMMY.

ON THEIR WALK BACK TO THE CIRCUS, EMMETT ASKS SHELLY ABOUT LIFE IN ASHLAND AND ABOUT THE PEOPLE OF THE TOWN. SHELLY OBLIGES ENTHUSIASTICALLY, TELLING EMMETT ABOUT THE PEOPLE AND THE THINGS TO DO AND SEE IN ASHLAND. SHELLY DOESN'T NOTICE EMMETT PICKING THE BOUQUET OF DAISIES FOR HER. NEITHER OF THEM NOTICE THAT THEY ARE BEING CLOSELY WATCHED AND FOLLOWED.

EMMETT REMOVES HIS HAT AND GOES TO PRESENT THE DAISIES TO SHELLY, JUST LIKE THE WAY HE'S SEEN THE LEADING MEN DO IN MOVIES. TOMMY MEYERS SEES SOMETHING ENITIRELY DIFFERENT. TO HIS EYES, EMMETT'S GESTURE LOOKS LIKE A SITUATION HE'D JUST READ ABOUT IN VAMPIRE BOOKS WHERE THE VAMPIRE CHARMS HIS PREY RIGHT BEFORE GOING IN FOR THE KILL. TOMMY ISN'T GOING TO LET THIS HAPPEN TO HIS SISTER IF HE CAN HELP IT.

"BACK TO **HELL** WITH YOU... **DEMON!!!**" TOMMY YELLS AS HE RUSHES EMMETT.

THE WOODEN SPIKE GOES INTO EMMETT'S HEART. THE LAST THING HE SEES IS THE FACE OF HATRED AND IGNORANCE. THE LAST THING HE HEARS IS HIS NAME.

"*NOOOOooooo*!!!!!!!!" SHELLY SCREAMS. "*EMMETT!!!*"

HIS LAST THOUGHTS ARE OF GOD.

"The fear of death follows from the fear of life. A man who lives fully is prepared to die at any time."

-Mark Twain

IN DEATH, MATERIAL POSSESSIONS HAVE NO USE OR MEANING, BUT FOR THE LIVING, IT'S THE EXPERIENCES ATTACHED TO THE POSSESSIONS THAT GIVE THEM MEANING. EVERY OBJECT HAS A STORY OR SENTIMENT. EMMETT'S CIRCUS FAMILY FILLS A CIGAR BOX WITH MEMENTOS OF THEIR EXPERIENCES WITH HIM.

THEY PLACE THE CIGAR BOX IN A TRUNK WITH EMMETT'S POSSESSIONS AND BURY IT SIX FEET SOUTH OF HIS BODY, WHICH IS UNDER A THRONE THEY BUILT FOR HIM, *"THE VAMPIRE PRINCE."*

MONDAY, SEPTEMBER 4, 1989. LABOR DAY.

BILLY, MIKE, AND PETE MAKE THEIR WAY THROUGH THE HILLS AND BACK INTO TOWN.

"MAN, I HOPE MY DAD DOESN'T KILL ME," SAYS BILLY. *"I TOTALLY* BELIEVED IT WHEN I PROMISED HIM I'D BE BACK IN TIME TO HELP WITH THE BBQ."

"NAH, MAN, I THINK HE'LL BE *JAZZED* AT SEEING THIS *TRUNK* WE FOUND," SAYS MIKE.

THE GUYS FINALLY MAKE IT BACK TO BILLY'S HOUSE. THE BACKYARD IS FILLED WITH FAMILY, FRIENDS AND NEIGHBORS.

"HEY! SORRY WE'RE *LATE,"* SAYS BILLY. "WE TRIED TO GET HERE ON TIME, BUT THIS *TRUNK* WE FOUND *BURIED* TOOK US A WHILE TO LUG BACK."

"BURIED?" BILLY'S MOM ASKS. "THAT PROBABLY *BELONGS* TO SOMEONE. WERE THERE ANY *LABELS* OR ANYTHING WITH A *NAME* OR *ADDRESS?"*

"THERE'S THIS TORN, FADED ONE *HERE.* WE DIDN'T REALLY GIVE IT A *LOOK,"* SAYS PETE. *"LEMME CHECK IT OUT…"*

"HMMM… IT'S HARD TO MAKE OUT…" PETE CONTINUES. *"…BUT, IT LOOKS LIKE IT SAYS *BEN THOMPSON.* THEN THERE'S AN ADDRESS…"

"DAD?" BILLY'S MOM SAYS, CONFUSED. "THAT'S…*YOUR* NAME."

"BEN!" SAYS BILLY'S GRANDMOTHER. *"IT'S OUR…* OUR.."

CRASH!!!

"GRANDMA!" BILLY SHOUTS. *"ARE YOU OKAY?!"*

I received much help and support from friends and family
as I toiled on *THE GRAVE*, for that I would like to thank:

Briana Fraga, Phred Jackson, Michael Gomez,
Pete Bresciani, Dan McCormack, Chris Bishop, Audu Paden,
my kids, and the number one, GOD.

THE GRAVE

A STEP-BY-STEP TOUR BY DAN FRAGA OF *THE GRAVE* AND HOW IT CAME TO BE.

SLAM'S CIRCUS *Development* — ADMIT ONE

Welcome to the supplemental portion of *The Grave*, where I will give you some insight into the process and origin of this book.

As I wrote in the introduction, I had a limited amount of time every day to work on *The Grave*. At first I thought of drawing the whole thing in a small Moleskine daily planner.

Here I tried out some early versions of the tree, and also what young Emmett would look like.

I had figured out a process in the book that seemed to work for what I wanted, though I'd run into some problems with the paper itself—the colors tended to bleed too much when I applied it with the wash. Here is a step-by-step of the progression from pencils to inks and color, featuring an early version of Moses the Mystic.

Then I discovered blank trading cards. Not only could they take all media, they were also the right size for what I needed—problem solved.

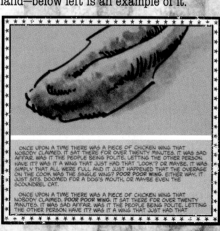

Originally I considered lettering by hand—below left is an example of it.

I realized I wasn't very good at lettering and opted to do it digitally. Not only would it look better but it would save time on corrections later.

Enter the Dan Fraga font. I commissioned this from Comicraft back in the late '90s for my book *The Gear Station*, and it represented a cleaned up version of my handwriting—to the far right is an early test I did.

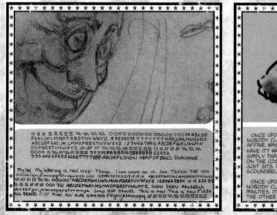

Once I worked out the details on how I would approach the story I needed to pick a start date—that day was January 1, 2014. Then I went on my social-media platforms and made an announcement about the book and my plan. The commitment was simple: a panel a day for the entire year—no going back after that.

In my postings I related that the book would be in black and white, with the exception of panels I would do on Sundays; those were to be in color to honor the old Sunday comic sections in newspapers.

Here are the pencils to the very first panel of *The Grave* along with the completed panel. You can tell that I was excited.

Something I have often done in my stories is to feature my hometown of Martinez.

I did it in the late '90s with *Kid Supreme*, and I certainly had to be sure to do it in *The Grave*. As a kid, one of the places I bought comic books from was a corner market called Case's. My pals and I would pretty much go there every day after school in 8th grade.

One of the most important places in my entire life is my grandparents' house. I learned how to draw there too, so it was only natural that I included it in *The Grave*.

Then there is Franklin Ridge, one of the most magical places in my life. There you will find a magnificent oak tree along with a stone throne. I used to go there as a kid and was always filled with awe at their beauty, and wonder about "the Throne," and what its origins could be. I'd make up tons of stories, one of which you're holding in your hands.

Photos by Phred Jackson.

For *The Grave* I didn't write a traditional outline—I had it all in my head. Initially I thought I could just write it daily by the seat of my pants. Once I realized it needed more of a structured process I would occasionally, when I felt I needed it, thumbnail the week's panels on a napkin to work out the pacing.

I also miscalculated my production time... even though I was working on blank trading cards—for the way they took the wash and color, and to help speed me up—but it didn't always work out that way. I was spending more time than I should have on some panels—I'm crazy about details.

Speaking of details, I researched everything I could, including the comics that would be on the spinner rack at the time the boys would be shopping at Case's. Here is the step-by-step process of the spinner rack panel.

1989 was a very special year for me, for both music and comics. This single picture represents some of my fondest memories that year.

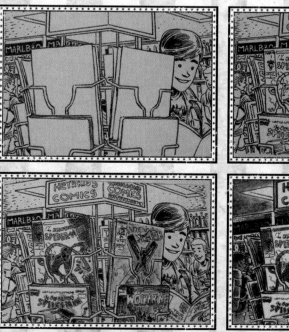

From time to time in *The Grave* I'd take reference photos to get the mood just right.
See if you can guess which panels these were for.

One of the ways I keep track of things in my life is by assigning meaning to objects or songs. In this story I decided to take that concept a step further. Each of the objects on this spread initially represented the seven deadly sins.

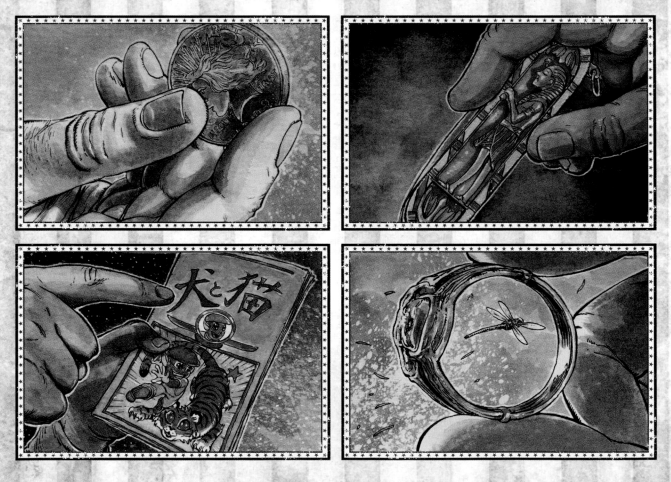

I wanted Emmett's life to have been full of all life had to offer, the good and the bad. Ultimately, the objects ended up only loosely signifying the deadly sins and, instead, wound up representing experiences he'd had. In the end, Emmett is buried with them.

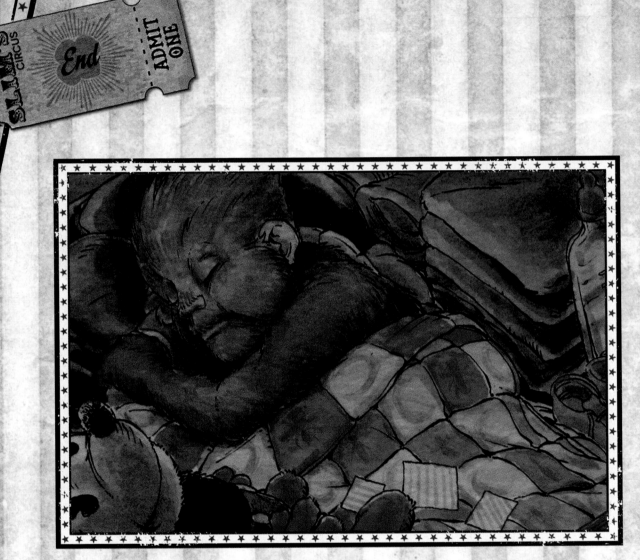

I began with a Mark Twain quote. "The fear of death follows
from the fear of life. A man who lives fully is prepared to die at any time."

This quote is what *The Grave* is all about to me. It is not intended
to be a tragic tale, but rather, one of a life fully lived.

Dan Fraga

THIS ENTIRE EFFORT IS DEDICATED TO THE
MAN WITHOUT WHOM I WOULD NEVER
HAVE LEARNED TO DRAW.

EMMETT JAY RYON
(1917-2014)